SIGHTSEEING

SIGHTSEEING

Stories

Rattawut Lapcharoensap

VIKING
CANADA

VIKING CANADA

Published by the Penguin Group

Penguin Group (Canada), 10 Alcorn Avenue, Toronto, Ontario, Canada M4V 3B2
(a division of Pearson Penguin Canada Inc.)
Penguin Group (USA) Inc., 375 Hudson Street, New York, New York 10014, U.S.A.
Penguin Books Ltd, 80 Strand, London WC2R 0RL, England
Penguin Ireland, 25 St Stephen's Green, Dublin 2, Ireland (a division of Penguin Books Ltd)
Penguin Group (Australia), 250 Camberwell Road, Camberwell, Victoria 3124, Australia
(a division of Pearson Australia Group Pty Ltd)
Penguin Books India Pvt Ltd, 11 Community Centre, Panchsheel Park,
New Delhi – 110 017, India
Penguin Group (NZ), Cnr Airborne and Rosedale Roads, Albany, Auckland, New Zealand
(a division of Pearson New Zealand Ltd)
Penguin Books (South Africa) (Pty) Ltd, 24 Sturdee Avenue, Rosebank,
Johannesburg 2196, South Africa

Penguin Books Ltd, Registered Offices: 80 Strand, London WC2R 0RL, England

First published 2005
Simultaneously published in the U.S.A. by Grove Press, an imprint of Grove/Atlantic, Inc.,
841 Broadway, New York, NY 10003

1 2 3 4 5 6 7 8 9 10 (RRD)

Copyright © Rattawut Lapcharoensap, 2005

The stories in this collection have appeared in the following publications, sometimes in
slightly different form: "Farangs" in *Granta* and *Best New American Voices 2005*; "At the
Café Lovely" in *Zoetrope: All-Story*; "Sightseeing" in *Glimmer Train.*

Publisher's note: This book is a work of fiction. Names, characters, places and incidents
either are the product of the author's imagination or are used fictitiously, and any
resemblance to actual persons living or dead, events, or locales is entirely coincidental.

Manufactured in the U.S.A.

LIBRARY AND ARCHIVES CANADA CATALOGUING IN PUBLICATION

Lapcharoensap, Rattawut
Sightseeing / Rattawut Lapcharoensap.
Short stories.
ISBN 0-670-06389-4
I. Title.
PS3612.A75S44 2005   813'.6   C2004-906160-7

British Library Cataloguing in Publication data available
American Library of Congress Cataloguing in Publication data available

Visit the Penguin Group (Canada) website at **www.penguin.ca**

For my mother,

Siriwan Sriboonyapirat

It is no wonder if the Siamese are not in any great care about their Subsistence, and if in the evening there is heard nothing but singing in their houses.

Simon de La Loubère, *A New Historical Relation of the Kingdom of Siam* (1693)

CONTENTS

SIGHTSEEING

FARANGS

This is how we count the days. June: the Germans come to the Island—football cleats, big T-shirts, thick tongues—speaking like spitting. July: the Italians, the French, the British, the Americans. The Italians like pad thai, its affinity with spaghetti. They like light fabrics, sunglasses, leather sandals. The French like plump girls, rambutans, disco music, baring their breasts. The British are here to work on their pasty complexions, their penchant for hashish. Americans are the fattest, the stingiest of the bunch. They may pretend to like pad thai or grilled prawns or the occasional curry, but twice a week they need their culinary comforts, their hamburgers and their pizzas. They're also the worst drunks. Never get too close to a drunk American. August brings the Japanese. Stay close to them. Never underestimate the power of the yen. Everything's cheap with imperial monies in hand and they're too polite to bargain. By the end of August, when the monsoon starts to blow, they're all consorting, slapping each other's backs, slipping each other drugs, sleeping with each other, sipping their liquor under the pink lights of the Island's bars. By September they've all deserted, leaving the Island to the Aussies and the Chinese, who are so omnipresent one need not mention them at all.

Ma says, "Pussy and elephants. That's all these people want." She always says this in August, at the season's peak, when she's tired of farangs running all over the Island, tired of finding used condoms in the motel's rooms, tired of guests complaining to her in five languages. She turns to me and says, "You give them history, temples, pagodas, traditional dance, floating markets, seafood curry, tapioca desserts, silk-weaving cooperatives, but all they really want is to ride some hulking gray beast like a bunch of wildmen and to pant over girls and to lie there half-dead getting skin cancer on the beach during the time in between."

We're having a late lunch, watching television in the motel office. The Island Network is showing *Rambo: First Blood Part II* again. Sylvester Stallone, dubbed in Thai, mows down an entire VC regiment with a bow and arrow. I tell Ma I've just met a girl. "It might be love," I say. "It might be real love, Ma. Like Romeo and Juliet love."

Ma turns off the television just as John Rambo flies a chopper to safety.

She tells me it's just my hormones. She sighs and says, "Oh no, not again. Don't be so naïve," she says. "I didn't raise you to be stupid. Are you bonking one of the guests? You better not be bonking one of the guests. Because if you are, if you're bonking one of the guests, we're going to have to bleed the pig. Remember, luk, we have an agreement."

I tell her she's being xenophobic. I tell her things are different this time. But Ma just licks her lips and says once more that if I'm bonking one of the guests, I can look forward to eating Clint Eastwood curry in the near future. Ma's always talking about killing my pig. And though I know she's just teasing, she says it with such zeal and a peculiar glint in her eyes that I run out to the pen to check on the swine.

I knew it was love when Clint Eastwood sniffed her crotch earlier that morning and the girl didn't scream or jump out of the sand or swat the pig like some of the other girls do. She merely lay there, snout in crotch, smiling that angelic smile, like it was the most natural thing in the world, running a hand over the fuzz of Clint Eastwood's head like he was some pink and docile dog, and said, giggling, "Why hello, oh my, what a nice surprise, you're quite a beast, aren't you?"

I'd been combing the motel beachfront for trash when I looked up from my morning chore and noticed Clint Eastwood sniffing his new friend. An American: Her Budweiser bikini told me so. I apologized from a distance, called the pig over, but the girl said it was okay, it was fine, the pig could stay as long as he liked. She called me over and said I could do the same.

I told her the pig's name.

"That's adorable," she said, laughing.

"He's the best," I said. "*Dirty Harry. Fistful of Dollars. The Outlaw Josey Wales. The Good, the Bad and the Ugly.*"

"He's a very good actor."

"Yes. Mister Eastwood is a first-class thespian."

Clint Eastwood trotted into the ocean for his morning bath then, leaving us alone, side-by-side in the sand. I looked to make sure Ma wasn't watching me from the office window. I explained how Clint Eastwood loves the ocean at low tide, the wet sand like a three-kilometer trough of mud. The girl sat up on her elbows, watched the pig, a waterlogged copy of *The Portrait of a Lady* at her side. She'd just gone for a swim and the beads of water on her navel seemed so close that for a moment I thought I might faint if I did not look away.

"I'm Elizabeth. Lizzie."

"Nice to meet you, Miss Elizabeth," I said. "I like your bikini."

She threw back her head and laughed. I admired the shine of her tiny, perfectly even rows of teeth, the gleam of that soft, rose-colored tongue quivering between them like the meat of some magnificent mussel.

"Oh my," she said, closing that mouth, gesturing with her chin. "I think your pig is drowning."

Clint Eastwood was rolling around where the ocean meets the sand, chasing receding waves, running away from oncoming ones. It's a game he plays every morning, scampering back and forth across the water's edge, and he snorted happily every time the waves knocked him into the foam.

"He's not drowning," I said. "He's swimming."

"I didn't know pigs could swim."

"Clint Eastwood can."

She smiled, a close-mouthed grin, admiring my pig at play, and I would've given anything in the world to see her tongue again, to reach out and sink my fingers into the hollows of her collarbone, to stare at that damp, beautiful navel all day long.

"I have an idea, Miss Elizabeth," I said, getting up, brushing the sand from the seat of my shorts. "This may seem rather presumptuous, but would you like to go for an elephant ride with me today?"

Ma doesn't want me bonking a farang because once, long ago, she had bonked a farang herself, against the wishes of her own parents, and all she got for her trouble was a broken heart and me in return. The farang was a man known to me only as Sergeant Marshall Henderson. I remember the Sergeant well, if only because he insisted I call him by his military rank.

"Not Daddy," I remember him saying in English, my first and only language at the time. "Sergeant. Sergeant Henderson. Sergeant Marshall. Remember you're a soldier now, boy. A spy for Uncle Sam's army."

And during those early years—before he went back to America, promising to send for us—the Sergeant and I would go on imaginary missions together, navigating our way through the thicket of farangs lazing on the beach.

"Private," he'd yell after me. "I don't have a good feeling about this, Private. This place gives me the creeps. We should radio for reinforcements. It could be an ambush."

"Let 'em come, Sergeant! We can take 'em!" I would squeal, crawling through the sand with a large stick in hand, eyes trained on the enemy. "Those gooks'll be sorry they ever showed their ugly faces."

One day, the three of us went to the fresh market by the Island's southern pier. I saw a litter of pigs there, six of them squeezed into a small cardboard box amidst the loud thudding of butchers' knives. I remember thinking of the little piglets I'd seen skewered and roasting over an open fire outside many of the Island's fancier restaurants.

I began to cry.

"What's wrong, Private?"

"I don't know."

"A soldier," the Sergeant grunted, "never cries."

"They just piggies," Ma laughed, bending to pat me on the back. Because of our plans to move to California, Ma was learning English at the time. She hasn't spoken a word of English to me since. "What piggies say, luk? What they say? Piggies say oink-oink. No cry, luk. No cry. Oink-oink is yummy-yummy."

A few days later, the Sergeant walked into my bedroom with something wriggling beneath his T-shirt. He sat down on the bed beside me. I remember the mattress sinking with his weight, the chirping of some desperate bird struggling in his belly.

"Congratulations, Private," the Sergeant whispered through the dark, holding out a young and frightened Clint Eastwood in one of his large, chapped hands. "You're a CO now. A commanding officer. From now on, you'll be responsible for the welfare of this recruit."

I stared at him dumbfounded, took the pig into my arms.

"Happy birthday, kiddo."

And shortly before the Sergeant left us, before Ma took over the motel from her parents, before she ever forbade me from speaking the Sergeant's language except to assist the motel's guests, before I knew what "bastard" or "mongrel" or "slut" or "whore" meant in any language, there was an evening when I walked into the ocean with Clint Eastwood—I was teaching him how to swim—and when I looked back to shore I saw my mother sitting between the Sergeant's legs in the sand, the sun a bright red orb on the crest of the mountains behind them. They spoke without looking at each other, my mother reaching back to hook an arm around his neck, while my piglet thrashed in the sea foam.

"Ma," I asked a few years later, "you think the Sergeant will ever send for us?"

"It's best, luk," Ma said in Thai, "if you never mention his name again. It gives me a headache."

After I finished combing the beach for trash, put Clint Eastwood back in his pen, Lizzie and I went up the mountain on my motorcycle to Surachai's house, where his uncle Mongkhon ran an elephant-trekking business. MR. MONGKHON'S JUNGLE SAFARI, a painted sign declared in their driveway. COME EXPERIENCE THE NATURAL BEAUTY OF FOREST WITH THE AMAZING VIEW OF OCEAN AND SPLENDID HORIZON FROM ELEPHANT'S BACK! I'd informed Uncle Mongkhon once that his sign was grammatically incorrect and that I'd lend him my expertise for a small fee, but he just laughed and said farangs preferred it just the way it was, thank you very much, they thought it was charming, and did I really think I was the only huakhuai who knew English on this godforsaken Island? During the war in Vietnam, before he started the business, Uncle Mongkhon had worked at an airbase on the mainland dishing lunch to American soldiers.

From where Lizzie and I stood, we could see the gray backs of two bulls peeking over the roof of their one-story house. Uncle Mongkhon used to have a corral full of elephants before the people at Monopolated Elephant Tours came to the Island and started underpricing the competition, monopolizing mountain-pass tariffs, and staking their claim upon farangs at hotels three stars and up—doing, in short, what they had done on so many other islands like ours. MET was putting Uncle Mongkhon out of business, and in the end he was forced to sell several elephants to logging companies on the mainland. Where there had once been eight elephants roaming the wide corral, now there were only two—Yai and Noi—aging bulls with ulcered bellies and flaccid trunks that hung limply between their crusty forelegs.

"Oh, wow," Lizzie said. "Are those actual elephants?"

I nodded.

"They're so huge."

She clapped a few times, laughing.

"Huge!" she said again, jumping up and down. She turned to me and smiled.

Surachai was lifting weights in the yard, a barbell in each hand. Uncle Mongkhon sat on the porch bare-chested, smoking a cigarette. When Surachai saw Lizzie standing there in her bikini, his arms went limp. For a second I was afraid he might drop the weights on his feet.

"Where'd you find this one?" he said in Thai, smirking, walking toward us.

"Boy," Uncle Mongkhon yelled from the porch, also in Thai. "You irritate me. Tell that girl to put on some clothes. You know damn well I don't let bikinis ride. This is a respectable establishment. We have rules."

"What are they saying?" Lizzie asked. Farangs get nervous when you carry on a conversation they can't understand.

"They just want to know if we need one elephant or two."

"Let's just get one." Lizzie smiled, reaching out to take my hand. "Let's ride one together." I held my breath. Her hand shot bright, surprising comets of heat up my arm. I wanted to yank my hand away even as I longed to stand there forever with our sweaty palms folded together. I heard the voice of Surachai's mother coming from inside the house, the light sizzle of a frying pan.

"It's nothing, Maew," Uncle Mongkhon yelled back to his sister inside. "Though I wouldn't come out here unless you like nudie shows. The mongrel's here with another member of his international harem."

"These are my friends," I said to Lizzie. "This is Surachai."

"How do you do," Surachai said in English, shaking her hand, looking at me all the while.

"I'm fine, thank you." Lizzie chuckled. "Nice to meet you."

"Yes yes yes," Surachai said, grinning like a fool. "Honor to meet you, madam. It will make me very gratified to let you ride my elephants. Very gratified. Because he"—Surachai patted me on the back now—"he my handsome soulmate. My best man."

Surachai beamed proudly at me. I'd taught him that word: "soulmate."

"You're married?" Lizzie asked. Surachai laughed hysterically, uncomprehendingly, widening his eyes at me for help.

"He's not," I said. "He meant to say 'best friend.'"

"Yes yes," Surachai said, nodding. "Best friend."

"You listening to me, boy?" Uncle Mongkhon got up from the porch and walked toward us. "Bikinis don't ride. It scares the animals."

"Sawatdee, Uncle," I said, greeting him with a wai, bending my head extra low for effect; but he slapped me on the head with a forehand when I came up.

"Tell the girl to put on some clothes," Uncle Mongkhon growled. "It's unholy."

"Aw, Uncle," I pleaded. "We didn't bring any with us."

"Need I remind you, boy, that the elephant is our national symbol? Sometimes I think your stubborn farang half keeps you from understanding this. You should be ashamed of yourself. I would tell your ma if it wouldn't break her heart.

"What if I went to her country and rode a bald eagle in my underwear, huh?" he continued, pointing at Lizzie. "How would she like it? Ask her, will you?"

"What's he saying?" Lizzie whispered in my ear.

"Ha ha ha," Surachai interjected, gesticulating wildly. "Everything okay, madam. Don't worry, be happy. My uncle, he just say elephants very terrified of your breasts."

"You should've told me to put on some clothes." Lizzie turned to me, frowning, letting go of my hand.

"It's really not a problem," I said, laughing.

"No," Uncle Mongkhon said to Lizzie in English. "Not a big problem, madam. Just a small one."

In the end, I took off my T-shirt and gave it to Lizzie. As we made our way toward the corral, I caught her grinning at the sight of my bare torso. Though I had been spending time at the new public gym by the pier, I felt some of that old adolescent embarrassment returning again. I casually flexed my muscles in the postures I'd practiced before my bedroom mirror so Lizzie could see my body not as the soft, skinny thing that it was, but as a pillar of strength and stamina.

When we came upon the gates of the elephant corral, Lizzie took my hand again. I turned to smile at her and she seemed, at that moment, some ethereal angel come from heaven to save me, an angel whose breasts left round, dark damp spots on my T-shirt. And when we mounted the elephant Yai, the beast rising quickly to his feet, Lizzie squealed and wrapped her arms so tightly around my bare waist that I would've gladly forfeited breathing for the rest of my life.

Under that jungle canopy, climbing up the mountainside on Yai's back, I told her about Sergeant Henderson, the motel, Ma, Clint Eastwood. She told me about her Ohio childhood, the New York City skyline, NASCAR, TJ Maxx, the drinking habits of American teenagers. I told her about Pamela, my last American girlfriend, and how she promised me her heart but never answered any of my letters. Lizzie nodded sympathetically and told me about her bastard boyfriend Hunter, whom she'd left last night at their hotel on the other side of the Island after finding him in the arms of a young prostitute. "That fucker," she said. "That whore." I told Lizzie she should forget about him, she deserved better, and besides Hunter was a stupid name anyway, and we both shook our heads and laughed at how poorly our lovers had behaved.

We came upon a scenic overlook. The sea rippled before us like a giant blue bedspread. I decided to give Yai a rest. He sat down gratefully on his haunches. For a minute Lizzie and I just sat there on the elephant's back looking out at the ocean, the wind blowing through the trees behind us. Yai was winded from the climb; we rose and fell with his heavy breaths. I told Lizzie about how the Sergeant and my mother used to stand on the beach, point east, and tell me that if I looked hard enough I might be able to catch a glimpse of the California coast rising out of the Pacific horizon. I pointed to Ma's motel below, the twelve bungalows like tiny insects on a golden shoreline. It's amazing, I told Lizzie, how small my life looks from such a height.

Lizzie hummed contentedly. Then she stood up on Yai's back.

"Here's your shirt," she said, tossing it at me.

With a quick sweeping motion, Lizzie took off her bikini top. Then she peeled off her bikini bottom. And then there she was—my American angel—naked on the back of Uncle Mongkhon's decrepit elephant.

"Your country is so hot," she said, smiling, crawling toward me on all fours. Yai made a low moan and shifted beneath us.

"Yes, it is," I said, pretending to study the horizon, rubbing Yai's parched, gray back.

After *Rambo*, lunch with my mother, and a brief afternoon nap, I walk out the door to meet Lizzie at the restaurant when Ma asks me what I'm all dressed up for.

"What do you mean?" I ask innocently, and Ma says, "What do I mean? Am I your mother? Are you my son? Are those black pants? Is that a button-down shirt? Is that the silk tie I bought for your birthday?"

She sniffs my head.

"And is that my nice mousse in your hair? And why," she asks, "do you smell like an elephant?"

I just stand there blinking at her questions.

"Don't think I don't know," she says finally. "I saw you, luk. I saw you on your motorcycle with that farang slut in her bikini."

I laugh and tell her I have hair mousse of my own. But Ma's still yelling at me when I go to the pen to fetch Clint Eastwood.

"Remember whose son you are," she says through the day's last light, standing in the office doorway with her arms akimbo. "Remember who raised you all these years."

"What are you talking about, Ma?"

"Why do you insist, luk, on chasing after these farangs?"

"You're being silly, Ma. It's just love. It's not a crime."

"I don't think," Ma says, "that I'm the silly one here, luk. I'm not the one taking my pet pig out to dinner just because some farang thinks it's cute."

I make my way down the beach with Clint Eastwood toward the lights of the restaurant. It's an outdoor establishment with low candlelit tables set in the sand and a large pit that the bare-chested chefs use to grill the day's catch. The restaurant's quite popular with the farangs. Wind at their backs, sand at their feet, night sky above, eating by the light of the moon and the stars. It's romantic, I suppose. Although I'm hesitant to spend so much money on what Ma calls second-rate seafood in a third-rate atmosphere, Lizzie suggested we meet there for dinner tonight, so who am I to argue with love's demands?

When we get to the restaurant, Lizzie's seated at one of the tables, candlelight flickering on her face. Clint Eastwood races ahead and nuzzles his snout in her lap, but Lizzie's face doesn't light up the way it did this morning. The other customers turn around in their seats to look at Clint Eastwood, and Lizzie seems embarrassed to be the object of his affections.

"Hi," she says when I get to the table, lighting a cigarette.

I kiss one of her hands, sit down beside her. I tell Clint Eastwood to stay. He lies down on his belly in the sand, head resting between his stubby feet. The sun is setting behind us, rays flickering across the plane of the sea, and I think I'm starting to understand why farangs come such a long way to get to the Island, why they travel so far to come to my home.

"Beautiful evening," I say, fingering the knot of my tie.

Lizzie nods absentmindedly.

"Is there something wrong?" I finally ask, after the waiter takes our order in English. "Have I done anything to offend you?"

Lizzie sighs, stubs out her cigarette in the bamboo ashtray.

"Nothing's wrong," she says. "Nothing at all."

But when our food arrives, Lizzie barely touches it. She keeps passing Clint Eastwood pieces of her sautéed prawns. Clint Eastwood gobbles them up gratefully. At least he's enjoying the meal, I think. On weekend nights, I often bring Clint Eastwood to this restaurant, after the tables have been stowed away, and he usually has to fight with the strays that descend on the beach for leftovers farangs leave in their wake: crab shells, fish bones, prawn husks.

"Something's wrong," I say. "You're not happy."

She lights another cigarette, blows a cloud of smoke.

"Hunter's here," she says finally, looking out at the darkening ocean.

"Your ex-boyfriend?"

"No," she says. "My boyfriend. He's here."

"Here?"

"Don't turn around. He's sitting right behind us with his friends."

At that moment, a large farang swoops into the empty seat across the table from us. He's dressed in a white undershirt and a pair of surfer's shorts. His nose is caked with sunscreen. His chest is pink from too much sun. There's a Buddha dangling from his neck. He looks like a deranged clown.

He reaches over and grabs a piece of stuffed squid from my plate.

"Who's the joker?" he asks Lizzie, gnawing on my squid. "Friend of yours?"

"Hunter," Lizzie says. "Please."

"Hey," he says, looking at me, taking another piece of squid from my entrée. "What's with the tie? And what's with the pig, man?"

I smile, put on a hand on Clint Eastwood's head.

"Hey you," he says. "I'm talking to you. Speak English? Talk American?"

He tears off a piece of squid with his front teeth. I can't stop staring at his powdered nose, the bulge of his hairy, sun-burned chest. I'm hoping he chokes.

"You've really outdone yourself this time, baby," he says to Lizzie now. "But that's what I love about you. Your unpredictability. Your wicked sense of humor. Didn't know you went for mute tards with pet pigs."

"Jesus."

"Oh, Lizzie," he says, feigning tenderness, reaching out to take one of her hands. "I've missed you so much. I hate it when you just leave like that. I've been worried sick about you. I'm sorry about last night, okay baby? Okay? I'm really sorry. But it was just a misunderstanding, you know? Jerry and Billyboy over there can testify to my innocence. You know how Thai girls get when we're around."

"We can talk about this later, Hunter."

"Yes," I interject. "I think you should talk to her later."

He just stares at me with that stupid white nose jutting out between his eyes. For a second, I think Hunter might throw the squid at me. But then he just pops the rest into his mouth, turns to Lizzie, and says with his mouth full:

"You fucked this joker, didn't you?"

I look over at Lizzie. She's staring at the table, tapping her fingers lightly against the wood. It seems she's about to cry. I stand up, throw a few hundred bahts on the table. Clint Eastwood follows my lead, rises clumsily to his feet.

"It was a pleasure meeting you, Miss Elizabeth," I say, smiling. I want to take her hand and run back to the motel so we can curl up together on the beach, watch the constellations. But Lizzie just keeps on staring at the top of that table.

I walk with Clint Eastwood back to the motel. We're the only ones on the beach. Night is upon us now. In the distance, I can see squidding boats perched on the horizon, searchlights luring their catch to the surface. Clint Eastwood races ahead, foraging for food in the sand, and I'm thinking with what I suppose is grief about all the American girls I've ever loved. Girls with names like Pamela, Angela, Stephanie, Joy. And now Lizzie.

One of the girls sent me a postcard of Miami once. A row of palm trees and a pink condo. "Hi Sweetie," it said. "I just wanted to say hi and to thank you for showing me a good time when I was over there. I'm in South Beach now, it's Spring Break, and let me tell you it's not half as beautiful as it is where you are. If you ever make it out to the U S of A, look me up okay?" which was nice of her, but she never told me where to look her up and there was no return address on the

postcard. I'd taken that girl to see phosphorescence in one of
the Island's bays and when she told me it was the most miraculous thing she'd ever seen, I told her I loved her—but the
girl just giggled and ran into the sea, that phosphorescent blue
streaking like a comet's tail behind her. Every time they do
that, I swear I'll never love another, and I'm thinking about
Lizzie and Hunter sitting at the restaurant now, and how this
is really the last time I'll let myself love one of her kind.

Halfway down the beach, I find Surachai sitting in a
mango tree. He's hidden behind a thicket of leaves, straddling
one of the branches, leaning back against the trunk.

When we were kids, Surachai and I used to run around
the beach advertising ourselves as the Island's Miraculous
Monkey Boys. We made loincloths out of Uncle Mongkhon's
straw heap and an old T-shirt Ma used as a rag. For a small
fee, we'd climb up trees and fetch coconuts for farangs, who
would ooh and aah at how nimble we were. A product of our
Island environment, they'd say, as if it was due to something
in the water and not the fact that we'd spent hours practicing
in Surachai's backyard. For added effect, we'd make monkey
noises when we climbed, which always made them laugh. They
would often be impressed, too, by my facility with the English
language. In one version of the speech I gave before every per-
formance, I played the part of an American boy shipwrecked
on the Island as an infant. With both parents dead, I was raised
in the jungle by a family of gibbons. Though we've long out-
grown what Ma calls "that idiot stunt," Surachai still comes

down from the mountain occasionally to climb a tree on the beach. He'll just sit there staring at the ocean for hours. It's meditative, he told me once. And the view is one-of-a-kind.

"You look terrible," he says now. "Something happen with that farang girl?"

I call Clint Eastwood over. I tell the pig to stay. I take off my leather shoes, my knitted socks, and—because I don't want to ruin them—the button-down shirt and the silk tie, leaving them all at the bottom of the trunk before joining Surachai on an adjacent branch. As I climb, the night air warm against my skin, I'm reminded of how pleasurable this used to be—hoisting myself up by my bare feet and fingertips—and I'm surprised by how easy it still is.

When I settle myself into the tree, I start to tell Surachai everything, including the episode on the elephant. As I talk, Surachai snakes his way out onto one of the branches and drops a mango for Clint Eastwood down below.

"At least you're having sex," Surachai says. "At least you're doing it. Some of us just get to sit in a mango tree and think about it."

I laugh.

"I don't suppose," Surachai says, "you loved this girl?"

I shrug.

"You're a mystery to me, phuan," Surachai says, climbing higher now into the branches. "I've known you all these years, and that's the one thing I'll never be able to understand—why you keep falling for these farang girls. It's like you're crazy for heartache. Plenty of nice Thai girls around. Girls without plane tickets."

"I know. I don't think they like me, though. Something about the way I look. I don't think my nose is flat enough."

"That may be true. But they don't like me either, okay? And I've got the flattest nose on the Island."

We sit silently for a while, perched in that mango tree like a couple of sloths, listening to the leaves rustling around us. I climb up to where Surachai is sitting. Through the thicket, I see Clint Eastwood jogging out to meet a group of farangs making their way down the beach. I call out to him, tell him to stay, but my pig's not listening to me.

It's Hunter and his friends, laughing, slapping each other's backs, tackling each other to the sand. Lizzie's walking with them silently, head down, trying to ignore their antics. When she sees Clint Eastwood racing up to meet her, she looks to see if I'm around. But she can't see us from where she's standing. She can't see us at all.

"It's that fucking pig again!" Hunter yells.

They all laugh, make rude little pig noises, jab him with their feet. Clint Eastwood panics. He squeals. He starts to run. The American boys give chase, try to tackle him to the ground. Lizzie tells them to leave the pig alone, but the boys aren't listening. Clint Eastwood is fast. He's making a fool of them, running in circles one way, then the other, zigzagging back and forth through the sand. The more they give chase, the more Clint Eastwood eludes them, the more frustrated the boys become, and what began as jovial tomfoolery has now turned into some kind of bizarre mission for Hunter and his friends. Their chase becomes more orchestrated. The movements of their shadows turn strategic. They try to corner the pig, run him into a trap, but Clint Eastwood keeps on moving between them, slipping through their fingers like he's greased.

I can tell that Clint Eastwood's beginning to tire, though. He can't keep it up much longer. He's an old pig. I start to climb down from the mango tree, but Surachai grabs me by the wrist.

"Wait," he says.

Surachai climbs out to one of the branches. He reaches for a mango and with a quick sweeping motion throws the fruit out to the beach. It hits one of the boys squarely on the shoulder.

"What the fuck!" I hear the boy yell, looking in the direction of the tree, though he continues to pursue Clint Eastwood.

They have him surrounded now, encircled. There's no way out for my pig.

I follow Surachai's lead, grab as many mangoes as I can. Our mangoes sail through the night air. Some of them miss, but some meet their targets squarely in the face, on the head, in the abdomen. Some of the mangoes hit Lizzie by accident, but I don't really care anymore, I'm not really aiming. I'm climbing through that tree like a gibbon, swinging gracefully between the branches, grabbing any piece of fruit—ripe or unripe—that I can get my hands on. Surachai starts to whoop like a monkey and I join him in the chorus. They all turn in our direction then, the four farangs, trying to dodge the mangoes as they come.

It's then that I see Clint Eastwood scurry away unnoticed. I see my pig running into the ocean, his pink snout inching across the sea's dark surface, phosphorescence glittering around his head like a crown of blue stars, and as I'm throwing each mango with all the strength I have, I'm thinking: Swim, Clint, Swim.

AT THE CAFÉ LOVELY

Every so often I dream of my brother's face on fire, his brown eyes—eyes very much like my own—staring at me through a terrible mask of flames. I wake to the scent of burning flesh, his fiery face looming before me as an afterimage, and in that darkness I am eleven again. I have not yet learned to trespass. I have not yet learned to grieve. Nor have I learned to pity us—my brother, my mother, and me—and Anek and I are in Bangkok sitting on the roof of our mother's house smoking cigarettes, watching people drifting by on their bicycles while the neighbors release their mangy dogs for the night to roam the city's streets.

It was a Saturday. Saturdays meant the city didn't burn the dump behind our house. We could breathe freely again. We wouldn't have to shut all the windows to keep out the stench, sleep in suffocating heat. Downstairs, we could hear Ma cooking in the outdoor kitchen, the clang of pots and pans, the warm smell of rice curling up toward us.

"Hey, kid," Anek said, stubbing his cigarette on the corrugated tin roof. "What's for dinner?" I sniffed the air. I had a keen sense of smell in those days. *Like a dog,* Anek told his friends once. *My little brother can smell your ma taking a crap on the other side of town.*

"Rice."

"Sure."

"Green beans. Fried egg."

"No meat?"

"No. I don't smell any meat."

"Oi." Anek threw a leaf over the edge of the roof. It hovered for a second before dropping swiftly to the street. "I'm tired of this. I'm tired of green beans."

Our father had been dead for four months. The insurance money from the factory was running out. There had been a malfunctioning crane and a crate the size of our house full of little wooden toys waiting to be sent to the children of America. Not a very large crate when I think about the size of the house, but big enough to kill a man when it fell on him from a height of ten meters. At the funeral, I was surprised by how little sadness I'd felt, as if it wasn't our father laid out before the mourners at all—wasn't him lying there in that rubberwood box, wasn't his body popping and crackling in the temple furnace like kindling—but a striking replica of our father in a state of rest. Pa had taken us to the wax museum once, and I remember thinking that he had somehow commissioned the museum to make a beautiful replica of himself and would be appearing any minute now at his own funeral.

After the cremation, we went with Ma to scatter the ashes at Pak Nam. We rode a small six-seater boat out to where the brown river emptied into the green sea. We leaned over the side—all three of us tipping the tiny tin urn together—while Ma tried to mutter a prayer through her tears.

Anek lit another cigarette.

"Are you going out tonight?" I asked.

"Yeah."

"Can I come with?"

"I don't think so."

"But you said last time—"

"Stop whining. I know what I said last time. I said I might. I said maybe. I made no promises, kid. I told you no lies. Last I checked, 'maybe' didn't mean 'yes.'"

A month before, for my birthday, Anek had taken me to the new American fast-food place at Sogo Mall. I was happy that day. I had dreamed all week of hamburgers and french fries and a nice cold soda and the air-conditioning of the place. During the ride to the mall, my arms wrapped around my brother's waist, the motorcycle sputtering under us, I imagined sitting at one of those shiny plastic tables across from my brother. We'd be pals. After all, it was my birthday—he had to grant me that. We would look like those university students I had seen through the floor-to-ceiling windows, the ones who laughed and sipped at their sodas. Afterward, we would walk into the summer sun with soft-serve sundaes, my brother's arm around my shoulder.

The place was packed, full of students and families clamoring for a taste of American fast food. All around us, people hungrily devoured their meals. I could smell beef cooking on the grill, hear peanut oil bubbling in the deep-fryers. I stared at the illuminated menu above the counter.

"What should I get, Anek?"

"Don't worry, kid. I know just what you'd like."

We waited in line, ordered at the counter, took our tray to an empty booth. Anek said he wasn't hungry, but I knew he had only enough money to order for me: a small burger and some fries. I decided not to ask him about it. I wasn't going to piss him off, what with it being my birthday and what with people being so touchy about money ever since Pa died. As we walked to the booth, I told Anek we could share the meal, I probably wouldn't be able to finish it all myself anyway.

Even though he had been telling me all month about how delicious and great the place was, my brother looked a little uncomfortable. He kept glancing around nervously. It occurred to me then that it was probably his first time there as well. We had on our best clothes that day—Anek in his blue jeans and white polo shirt, me in my khakis and red button-down— but even then I knew our clothes couldn't compare with the other kids' clothes. Their clothes had been bought in the mall; ours had been bought at the weekend bazaar and were cheap imitations of what they wore.

Anek stared across the table at me. He smiled. He tousled my hair. "Happy birthday, kid. Eat up."

"Thanks, Anek."

I unwrapped the burger. I peeked under the bun at the gray meat, the limp green pickles, the swirl of yellow mustard and red ketchup drenching the bun. Anek stared out the window at the road in front of the mall. For some reason, I suddenly felt like I should eat as quickly as possible so we could get the hell out of there. I didn't feel so excited anymore. And I noticed that the place smelled strange—a scent I'd never encountered before—a bit rancid, like palaa fish left too long in the sun. Later, I would find out it was cheese.

I took a few apprehensive bites at the bun. I bit into the brittle meat. I chewed and I chewed and I chewed and I finally swallowed, the thick mass inching slowly down my throat. I took another bite. Then I felt my stomach shoot up to my throat like one of those bottle rockets Anek and I used to set off in front of Apae's convenience store just to piss him off. I remember thinking, Oh fuck, oh fuck, please no, but before I could take a deep breath to settle things, it all came rushing out of me. I threw up all over that shiny American linoleum floor.

A hush fell over the place, followed by a smattering of giggles.

"Oh, you fucking pussy," Anek hissed.

"I'm sorry, Anek."

"You goddamn, motherfucking, monkey-cock-sucking piece of low-class pussy."

I wiped my lips with my forearm. Anek pulled me to my feet, led me out through the glass double doors, his hand on my collar. I tried to say sorry again, but before I could mouth the words my heart felt like it might explode and—just as we cleared the doors—I sent a stream of gray-green vomit splashing against the hot concrete.

"Oh. My. Fucking. Lord. Why?" Anek moaned, lifting his face to the sky. "Oh why, Lord? Why hast thou forsaken me?" Anek and I had been watching a lot of Christian movies on TV lately.

When we came to a traffic stop an hour later, I was leaning against my brother's back, still feeling ill, thick traffic smoke whipping around us. Anek turned to me and said: "That's the first and last time, kid. I can't believe you. All that money for a bunch of puke. No more fucking hamburgers for you."

We finished watching the sun set over the neighborhood, a panoply of red and orange and purple and blue. Anek told me that Bangkok sunsets were the most beautiful sunsets in the world. "It's the pollution," he said. "Brings out the colors in the sky." Then after Anek and I smoked the last of the cigarettes, we climbed down from the roof.

At dinner, as usual, we barely said a word to each other. Ma had been saying less and less ever since that crate of toys killed our father. She was all headshakes and nods, headshakes and nods. We picked at our green beans, slathered fish sauce on our rice.

"Thanks for the meal, Ma."

Ma nodded.

"Yeah, Ma, this is delicious."

She nodded again.

Besides the silence, Ma's cooking was also getting worse, but we couldn't bring ourselves to say anything about it. What's more, she had perfected the art of moving silently through the house. She seemed an apparition in those days. She'd retreated into herself. She no longer watched over us. She simply watched. I'd be doodling in my book at the kitchen table and all of a sudden Ma would just be sitting there, peering at me with her chin in one hand. Or Anek and I would be horsing around in the outdoor kitchen after dinner, throwing buckets of dirty dishwater on each other, and we'd look over our shoulders to find Ma standing against the crumbling concrete siding of the house. Anek told me she caught him masturbating in the bathroom once. He didn't even realize she had opened the door until he heard it shut, a loud slam so he could know that she'd seen him. Anek didn't masturbate for weeks after that and neither did I.

One night I caught Ma staring at the bedroom mirror with an astonished look on her face, as if she no longer recognized her own sallow reflection. It seemed Pa's death had made our mother a curious spectator of her own life, though when I think of her now I wonder if she was simply waiting for us to notice her grief. But we were just children, Anek and I, and when children learn to acknowledge the gravity of their loved ones' sorrows they're no longer children.

"That woman needs help," Anek said after we washed the dishes that evening.

"She's just sad, Anek."

"Listen, kid, I'm sad too, okay? Do you see me walking around like a mute, though? Do you see me sneaking around the house like I'm some fucking ninja?"

I dropped it. I didn't feel like talking about the state of things that night, not with Anek. I knew he would get angry if we talked about Pa, if we talked about his death, if we talked about what it was doing to Ma. I never knew what to do with my brother's anger in those days. I simply and desperately needed his love.

I think Anek felt bad about the hamburger incident because he started giving me lessons on the motorcycle, an old 350cc Honda our father had ridden to the factory every morning. After Pa died, Ma wanted to sell the bike, but Anek convinced her not to. He told her the bike wasn't worth much. He claimed it needed too many repairs. But I knew that aside from some superficial damage—chipped paint, an ugly crack in the rear mudguard, rusted-through places in the exhaust pipe—the bike was in fine working condition. Anek wanted the bike for himself. He'd been complaining all year about being the only one among his friends without a bike. We'd spent countless hours at the mall showroom, my brother wandering among the gleaming new bikes while I trailed behind him absentmindedly. And though I thought then that my brother had lied to my mother out of selfishness, I know now that Pa did not leave us much. That Honda was Anek's inheritance.

He'd kick-start it for me—I didn't have the strength to do it myself—and I'd hop on in front and ride slowly through the neighborhood with Anek behind me.

"I'll kill you, you little shit. I'll kill you if you break my bike," he'd yell when I approached a turn too fast or when I had trouble steadying the handlebars after coming out of one. "I'm gonna nail you to a fucking cross like Jesus-fucking-Christ."

My feet barely reached the gear pedal, but I'd learned, within a week, to shift into second by sliding off the seat. I'd accelerate out of first, snap the clutch, slide off the seat just so, then pop the gear into place. We'd putter by the city dump at twenty, twenty-five kilos an hour and some of the dek khaya, the garbage children whose families lived in shanties on the dump, would race alongside us, urging me to go faster, asking Anek if they could ride too.

I began to understand the way Anek had eyed those showroom bikes. I began to get a taste for speed.

"That's as fast as I'm letting you go," Anek once said when we got home. "Second gear's good enough for now."

"But I can do it, Anek. I can do it."

"Get taller, kid. Get stronger."

"C'mon, Anek. Please. Second is so slow. It's stupid."

"I'll tell you what's stupid, little brother. What's stupid is you're eleven years old. What's stupid is you go into turns like a drunkard. What's stupid is you can't even reach the gear pedal. Grow, kid. Give me twenty more centimeters. Then maybe we'll talk about letting you do third. Maybe."

"Why can't I come?"

"Because you can't, that's why."

"But you said last week—"

"I already told you, vomit-boy. I know what I said last week. I said maybe. Which part of that didn't you understand? I didn't say, 'Oh yes! Of course, buddy! I love you so much! You're my super pal! I'd love to take you out next Saturday!' now did I?"

"Just this once, Anek. I promise I won't bother you."

"I don't think so."

"Please?"

"'Please' nothing, little brother. Sit at home and watch a soap with Ma or something."

"But why, Anek? Why can't I go with you?"

"Because I'm going where grown men go, that's why. Because last I checked, last time I saw you naked, you were far from being grown."

"I promise I won't bother you, Anek. I'll just sit in a corner or something. Really. I promise. I'll stay out of your way. Just don't leave me here with Ma tonight."

* * *

When we were young, our mother would put on her perfume every evening before Pa came home. She would smell like jasmine, fresh-picked off a tree. Pa, he would smell of the cologne he dabbed on after he got out of the shower. Although I would never smell the ocean until we went out to Pak Nam to scatter his ashes, I knew that my father smelled like the sea. I just knew it. Anek and I would sit between them, watching some soap opera on TV, and I would inhale their scents, the scents of my parents, and imagine millions of tiny white flowers floating on the surface of a wide and green and bottomless ocean.

But those scents are lost to me now, and I've often wondered if, in my belated sorrow, with all my tardy regrets, I've imagined them all these years.

Anek finally gave in and took me. We rode out to Minburi District along the new speedway, the engine squealing beneath us. We were going so fast that my face felt stretched impossibly tight. I wanted to tell Anek to slow down but I remembered that I had promised to stay out of his way.

We were wearing our best clothes again that night, the same old outfits: Anek in his blue jeans and white polo shirt, me in my khakis and red button-down. When we walked out of the house Ma glanced up from the TV with a look that said *What are you all dressed up for?* and Anek told her he was taking me out to the new ice-skating rink, he heard it was all the rage. I even said, "Imagine that, Ma. Ice-skating in Bangkok," but she just nodded, her lips a straight thin line, and went back to watching television.

"'Imagine that, Ma' . . . ," Anek teased when we walked out.

"Eat shit, Anek."

"Whoa there. Be careful, little one. Don't make me change my mind."

When we arrived at the place, it was not what I had imagined at all. I expected mirror balls and multicolored lights and loud American music and hundreds of people dancing inside—like places I'd seen in the district west of our neighborhood, places all the farangs frequented at night. It didn't look like that. It was only a shophouse, like the thousands of tiny two-story shophouses all over the city—short and common, square and concrete, in need of a new paint job. A pink neon sign blinked in the tinted window. CAFÉ LOVELY, it said in English. I could hear the soft, muffled sounds of upcountry music reaching across the street.

"This is it?"

"I can take you home," Anek said. "That's not a problem."

The place smelled of mothballs. There was an old juke-box in the corner. A couple of girls in miniskirts and tank tops and heavy makeup danced and swayed with two balding, middle-aged local men. The men looked awkward with those girls in their arms, feet moving out of time, their large hands gripping the girls' slender waists. In a dark corner, more girls were seated at a table, laughing. They sounded like a flock of excited birds. I'd never seen so many girls in my life.

Three of Anek's friends were already at a table.

"What's with the baby-sitting?" one of them asked, grinning.

"Sorry," Anek said sheepishly as we sat down. "Couldn't bear to leave him home with my crazy ma."

"You hungry, kid?" said another. "Want a hamburger?"

"No thanks."

"Hey," Anek said. "Leave him alone. Let's just pretend he's not here."

The song ended. I saw a girl go up a set of stairs at the back, leading one of the men by the hand. I didn't even have to ask. I wondered if Anek, too, would be going up those stairs at the end of the night. And although I had been disappointed at first by the café's shoddy facade, I found myself excited now by its possibilities.

Anek must've seen me staring because he slapped me hard across the back of the head. "Ow," I cried, rubbing my head with a palm. "That fucking hurt."

"Keep your eyes to yourself, little man."

"That's right," one of his friends intoned, the one who'd asked me if I wanted a hamburger. "Be careful what you wish for, boy. The AIDS might eat your dick."

"Not before it eats your mom's, though," I replied, and they all laughed, even my brother, Anek, who said, "Awesome," and smiled at me for the first time all evening.

* * *

Anek had come home one night when I was nine and told me that Pa had taken him out for his fifteenth birthday. The city dump was burning; there was a light red glow in the sky from the pyre. Even though our windows were shut, I could still smell the putrid scent of tires and plastic and garbage burning, the sour odor seeping through our windows. I was sleeping in my underwear, two fans turned on high, both fixed in my direction. Anek walked into the room, stripped down to his underwear, and thrust out his hand.

"Bet you can't tell me what this smell is."

I sniffed his fingers. It smelled like awsuan: oysters simmered in egg yolk. But somehow I knew it wasn't food.

"What is it?"

Anek chuckled.

"What is it, Anek?"

"That, my dear brother, is the smell of"—he put his hand up to his face, sniffed it hungrily—"heaven."

I blinked at him.

"A woman, kid. You know what that is? Pa took me to a sophaeni tonight. And let me tell you, little one, when he takes you for your fifteenth birthday, you'll never be the same again. This scent"—he raised his hand to his face again—"it'll change your fucking life."

* * *

Anek and his friends had already poured themselves a few
drinks while I sat there sipping my cola—half listening to their
banter, half watching the girls across the room—when one of
Anek's friends stood up and said: "It's getting to that time of
night, guys."

I didn't know what the hell was going on, I just thought
he was a funny drunk, but then Anek got up and told the bartender we were going outside for a breath of fresh air. One of
the girls came up to us, put a hand on Anek's shoulder, and said,
"Leaving so soon?" but Anek told her not to worry, to be pa-
tient, he'd be back to give her what she wanted soon. The girl
winked at me and said, "Who's the handsome little boy?" and I
smiled back, but Anek had to be an asshole, so he said, "Oh,
that's my virgin brother," which annoyed me because no girl
had ever winked at me before and I thought she was beautiful.

I followed Anek and his friends out of the Café Lovely
and into a small alley off the shophouse row. Anek didn't want
to leave me by myself. He said it didn't look good—leaving a
little boy alone in a place like that—but I could tell that he
didn't want me to come, either. As we cut into the dark alley,
I had a feeling that a breath of fresh air was the last thing we
were going to get.

When we stopped, one of Anek's friends pulled out a
small container of paint thinner from a plastic bag. "All right,"
he said, prying at the lid with a small pocketknife. The lid flew
open with a loud pop and rolled down the dark alley, swirling
to a stop by a Dumpster. I saw the quick shadows of roaches

scattering in its wake. That's what the alley smelled like—roaches: dank and humid like the back room where Ma put away our father's belongings. Anek's friend poured half the can into the plastic bag, the liquid thick and translucent, the bag sagging from the weight, while the others flicked their cigarettes into the sewer ditch along the side of the alley. The thinner gave off a sharp, strong odor, punched little pinpricks in my nostrils, and reminded me of days when Pa and Anek used to fumigate the house. Anek's friend pulled out another plastic bag from his back pocket and put the first bag with the thinner inside of it.

"Okay." He held out the double bag with one hand, offering it to his friends, the way I'd seen butchers at the market holding dead chickens by the neck. I could hear the jukebox starting up again in the café, another old upcountry tune echoing softly down the alley. "Who's first?"

For a second, they all stood with their hands in their pockets. Then Anek reached out and took the bag with a quick, impatient gesture.

"Let's just get this over with," he said. "I tell you guys, though, one hit and I'm done. I don't like having my little brother around this shit."

I realized then what they were doing. I knew what huffers were, but I'd always imagined little kids and strung-out homeless guys in the Klong Toey slum with their heads buried in pots of rubber cement. I suddenly became very afraid—I wanted to grab the bag out of my brother's hands—even as I longed to watch Anek do it, wanted, in fact, to do it myself, to show Anek and his friends my indifference.

Anek brought the mouth of the bag to his chin. He took a big, deep breath, pulled his entire body back like it was a slingshot, then blew into the bag, inflating it like a balloon, the loose ends covering half his face, and it made a sound like a quick wind blowing through a sail. The bag grew larger and larger and I was afraid that it might burst, that the thinner would go flying everywhere. Anek looked at me the whole time he blew, his eyes growing wider and wider. He kept blowing and blowing and blowing, and I knew that my brother was blowing for a long time because one of the guys said, "Fucking inhale already, Anek," but he kept on blowing and blowing and all that time he kept looking at me with those eyes about to pop out of his head. I don't know what he was trying to tell me then, looking at me like that, but I remember noticing for the first time that he had our mother's eyes. He finally inhaled, sucked his breath back into his chest, the plastic balloon collapsing in on itself, and then my brother was blinking hard, teetering, like a boxer stunned by a swift and surprising blow, and I knew that whatever it was he had smelled, whatever scent he had just inhaled, it was knocking him off his feet. He handed the bag to one of the other guys and said, "C'mon kid, let's get out of here," and I followed my brother out of the dark alley, back into the dimly lit street.

Years later, I'd be in a different alley with friends of my own, and one of the guys, high off a can of spray paint, would absentmindedly light a cigarette after taking a hit and his face would burst into a sheet of blue flames. He ran around the alley wild with panic, running into the sides of the buildings, stumbling and falling and getting back to his feet again, hands flying violently around his burning face as if trying to beat back a swarm of attacking insects. He never made a sound, just ran around that alley with his face on fire in silent terror, the flames catching in his hair and his clothes, looking like some giant ignited match in the shape of a man. For a second, we couldn't quite comprehend what was happening—some of us laughed, most of us were just stunned—before I managed to chase the boy down, tackle him to the ground, and beat out the flames from his face with my T-shirt. His eyes were wild with terror and we just stared at each other for a moment before he started to weep hysterically, his body shaking under mine, the terrible scent of burnt flesh and singed hair filling the alley. His lashes and eyebrows had been burned cleanly off his face. His eyelids were raw, pink. His face began to swell immediately, large white welts blooming here and there. And he just kept on crying beneath me, calling for his mother and father, blubbering incoherently in the high, desperate voice of a child.

Back at the café, I could tell that the thinner was setting in. Anek kept tilting back in his seat, dilating his eyes. He took a long swig of his rye, poured himself another. I knew we wouldn't be going home for a while. The same girl who had winked at me earlier walked across the room and sat down at our table. She put her arm around my shoulder. I felt my body tense. She smelled like menthol, like the prickly heat powder Anek and I sprinkled on ourselves to keep cool at night.

"Hi, handsome."

"Hi."

I sipped at the last of my cola. Across the room, I noticed the girls looking our way, giggling among themselves.

"That's my brother," Anek drawled.

"I know, Anek."

"He's a little high," I said, laughing.

"Looks like it."

"Yeah." Anek smiled, slow and lazy. "Just a little."

"Where are the rest?" she asked me.

"Outside."

"What about you, handsome? Are you high?"

"No."

"Ever been?"

"Yeah. Of course. Plenty of times."

She laughed, threw her head far back. Menthol. I felt my heart pounding in my chest. I wanted to smear her carmine lips with my hands. I reached across the table for Anek's Krong Thips and lit one.

"You're adorable," she said, pinching one of my cheeks. I felt myself blush. "But you shouldn't be smoking those things at your age."

"I know," I said, smiling at her, taking a drag. "Cigarettes are bad."

"C'mon," Anek said, getting up abruptly, swaying a little bit. He reached out and grabbed her hand from my shoulder. "C'mon." He nodded toward the staircase. "Let's go."

She stood up, her hand dangling in my brother's, while I sat between them.

"What about the kid?" she asked, looking down at me.

"Oh, he'll be fine."

"Maybe not tonight, Anek. We shouldn't leave the kid by himself."

"Hey barf-boy," Anek said. "You gonna be okay?"

I looked up at my brother. He still had the girl's hand in his own. I took a long drag of my cigarette.

"Yeah. I'll be fine, Anek. I'm not a kid anymore."

Anek smiled as if he found me amusing. I wanted to wipe the smile off his face. I felt angry. I didn't want to be abandoned. Anek must've sensed this because there suddenly seemed something sad about my brother's smile. He dropped the girl's hand. He reached out and tapped me lightly on the head.

"Okay, kid. You don't have to be so tough all the time," he said finally. He took a deep breath, his voice a little steadier, his eyes a little wider. "Tell you what. I'm just gonna go put some music in the jukebox. Then Nong and I are gonna dance. Then we're gonna go upstairs for a while. Just a short while. We won't be long. I promise. Then, if you want, we'll go home, okay?" But I just took another drag of my cigarette, watched the girls in the corner, tried not to meet my brother's eyes.

She led him out to the dance floor. They stood by the jukebox and he slipped a few coins into the machine, steadying himself with one hand. A record came on, the sound of high Isan flutes and xylophones and a hand drum striking up the first few bars. Anek clumsily took one of the girl's hands, hooked an arm around her waist, and they started moving to the music. They stood close, their chins on each other's shoulders, though perhaps a little too close for the girl, because she leaned away from my brother a few times. But then again, maybe it was because my brother was high, drunk, and they kept losing their balance. They didn't look like dancers at all after a while; they looked like they were just holding each other up, falling into and out of each other's body.

I hadn't recognized the tune at first—I thought it was just another generic upcountry ballad—but then a woman's falsetto came soaring over the instruments and I remembered that it was an old record of Ma's, something she and Pa used to listen to in the early afternoon, hours before the endlessly growing mass of garbage burned behind our house. Those days curry and fish in tamarind sauce would be cooking on the stove, the aroma wafting into the house, and I swear that right then, listening to that music, I could smell it on the tip of my nose.

Oh beloved, so sad was my departure . . .

I looked at Anek and the girl. She couldn't have been more than sixteen years old—younger than my brother—but it seemed clear to me now that she was the one holding him up, directing his course, leading him. I wondered how many men she had held up tonight, how many more she would hold in the thousands of nights before her. I wondered whether she was already finding the force of their weight unbearable. I wondered whether I would be adding my weight to that mass one day. She held him close now and he, he pulled away, fell out of sync, though they continued to move across the floor as slowly and languorously as the music in the café.

. . . I am tired, I am broken, I am lost . . .

When the song ended, they pulled away from each other. Anek took the girl by the hand and led her toward the staircase. As they began to mount the stairs, the girl said something to my brother and they both stopped to look back at me. My brother smiled weakly then, raised a hand in my direction. I looked away, pretended not to see the gesture, stirring the ash in the tray with my cigarette. When I looked back they were gone.

The place fell silent. A balding, middle-aged man walked down the stairs. He made for the door, his steps quick and certain, as if he couldn't wait to leave. When he passed by my table, I caught a whiff of him, and his scent lingered on my nostrils for a while. He smelled like okra.

I stood up. I don't know why I walked toward that staircase. Perhaps it was childish curiosity. Or perhaps I wanted to see, once and for all, what secrets, what sins, what comforts those stairs led one to. Or perhaps I wanted to retrieve Anek before he did whatever it was I thought he might do.

I had imagined darkness and was surprised, when I arrived at the top of the stairs, to find a brightly lit hallway flanked on both sides by closed doors. The corridor smelled sweet, sickly, as if it had been perfumed to cover up some stench. The bare walls gleamed under the buzzing fluorescent fixtures. I heard another song start up downstairs, laughter again from the table of girls. I walked slowly down the hallway; the noises downstairs faded to a murmur. I felt like I had surfaced into another world and left those distant, muffled sounds beneath me, underwater. As I crept along, careful to be silent, I began to hear a chorus of ghostly, guttural groans coming from behind the doors. I heard a man whimper; I heard another cry out incoherently. After a while, those rooms seemed—with their grunting and moaning—like torture chambers in which faceless men suffered untold cruelties. I wondered if my brother was making any of these noises. I thought of the video Anek had borrowed from one of his friends, the women in them cooing and squealing perversely, and how strange it was now that none of the women could be heard. Instead, I could hear only the men, growling away as if in some terrible, solitary animal pain. I imagined the men writhing against the women, and I wondered how these women—those girls sitting downstairs—could possibly endure in such silence.

Just as I turned the corner, a hand grabbed me by the collar, choking me. I was certain, for a moment, that I would now be dragged into one of the rooms and made to join that chorus of howling men.

"Little boy," a voice hissed in my ear. "Where do you think you're going?"

It was the bartender from downstairs. He looked down at me, brow furrowed, beads of spittle glistening at the corners of his lips. I smelled whiskey on his breath, felt his large, chapped hands on my neck as he pulled me toward him and lifted me off the concrete floor.

"You're in the wrong place," he whispered into my ear, while I struggled against his grip. "I should kill you for being up here. I should snap your head right off your fucking neck."

I screamed for Anek then. I sent my brother's name echoing down that empty hallway. I screamed his name over and over again as the bartender lifted me up into his thick, ropy arms. The more I struggled against the bartender, the more dire my predicament seemed, and I cried out for my brother as I had never cried out before. The men seemed to stop their moaning then and, for a moment, I felt as if my cries were the only sound in the world. I saw a few doors open, a couple of women sticking out their heads to look at the commotion. The bartender walked backward with me, toward the staircase, as I kicked and struggled against his suffocating embrace.

Then I saw my brother hobbling in his underwear, his blue jeans shackling his feet.

"Hey!" Anek yelled, staggering, bending down to gather up his jeans. "Hey!" The man stopped, loosened his grip on my body. "Hey!" Anek yelled again, getting closer now. "That's my little brother, you cocksucker. Put him down."

The bartender still had me, his breath hot on my neck. As Anek struggled to pull up his jeans I glimpsed the purple, bulbous head of his penis peeking over the waistband of his underwear. The bartender must've seen this too; he began to chuckle obscenely.

"Get him out of here, Anek," he said. Anek nodded grimly. The bartender put me down, shoved me lightly toward my brother. "You know I can't have him up here," he said.

"You okay, kid?" Anek asked, breathless, ignoring the bartender, bending down to look me in the eyes. I saw the girl standing in the hallway behind Anek, a towel wrapped loosely around her small body. She waved at me, smiling, and then walked back into the room. The other women disappeared as well. I heard the bartender going downstairs, the steps creaking under his weight. Soon, Anek and I were the only people left in that hallway, and for some reason—despite my attempts to steel myself—I began to cry. I tried to apologize to my brother through the tears.

"Oh shit," my brother muttered, pulling me to his chest. "C'mon, kid," he said. "Let's just go home."

*   *   *

We went to the bathroom. I stood sniveling by a urinal while Anek leaned over a sink and dashed water on his face. When we came back out, his steps were no longer unsteady, though his voice still quavered slightly. Beads of water glistened on his face. He lit a cigarette at the door and waved to the bartender and the girls in the corner. I couldn't look at them now.

We stepped into the street. His friends were still in the alley, laughing and stumbling, flinging pieces of garbage from the Dumpster at each other. We stood at the mouth of the alley and Anek said, "See you later, boys," and one of the them yelled back, "Wait, Anek! Wait! I have an idea! Let's put your kid brother in the dump!" But Anek just put an arm around my shoulder and said, "Maybe next time."

We crossed the street. Anek kick-started the motorcycle. It sputtered and wheezed and coughed before settling into a soft, persistent purr. I started to climb onto the back, but Anek said, "What the hell are you doing? Can't you see I'm in no shape to take us home?"

"You can't be serious, Anek."

"Serious as our pa is dead, kid."

I stood there for a moment, dumbfounded. I climbed onto the front seat.

"I swear to God, though, you make so much as a dent on my bike and I'll—"

But I had already cocked the accelerator and we were on our way. Slowly, of course. I slipped off the seat a little so I could reach the pedal, snapped the clutch with my left hand, and popped the bike into second gear. We sputtered for a while like that along the streets of Minburi, crawling at fifteen kilos, until I made a sharp right onto the bridge that would take us out to the new speedway.

Years later, I would ask Anek if he remembered this night. He would say that I made it up. He never would've taken me to the Café Lovely at such a young age, he'd say, never would've let me drive that bike home. He denies it now because he doesn't want to feel responsible for the way things turned out, for the way we abandoned our mother to that hot and empty house, for the thoughtless, desperate things I would learn to do. Later that same year, my mother would wake me up in the middle of the night. She would be crying. She would ask me to sleep again in her bed. And, for the first time, I would refuse her. I would deny Ma the comfort of my body.

After Anek moved to an apartment across the river in Thonburi, I gathered my father's belongings from the back room and pawned them while Ma was at work. I used the money to buy myself a motorcycle. When I got home, my mother was waiting for me. She came at me with a thousand impotent fists, and when she was finished, spent and exhausted, her small body quivering in my arms, she asked me to leave her house. I did. And I did not return to that house again until it was too late, until Anek called to say our mother

was ill, that she wanted us by her side to accompany her
through her final hours.

That night, as we rode back from the Café Lovely, I felt my
brother's arms around my waist, his head slumped on my shoulder. I remember thinking then about how I'd never felt the
weight of my brother's head before. His hot, measured breaths
warmed my neck. I could still smell the thinner's faint, sour scent
wafting from his face. I suddenly became afraid that Anek had
fallen asleep and would tumble off the bike at any moment.

"Are you awake, Anek?"

"Yeah, I'm awake."

"Good."

"Do me a favor. Eyes on the road."

"I'm glad you're awake, Anek."

"Third."

"What's that?"

"I said third."

"You sure?"

"It's a onetime offer, little man."

I slipped off the seat, accelerated a little, twisted the
clutch, and tapped the gear pedal as we hit the speedway. I
was so excited we might as well have broken the sound bar-
rier, but the engine jolted us forward just enough that my grip
weakened and we went swerving along the empty speedway,
weaving wildly back and forth at thirty kilometers an hour.

"Easy now. Easy. There, there, you have it. Just take a deep breath now. Holy shit, I almost had to break your ass back there. You almost had us kissing the pavement."

I could feel the palms of my hands slick against the throttle. Even at thirty kilos, the wind blew hot against our faces.

"Accelerate," Anek said.

"No fucking way."

"I said accelerate. This is a speedway, you know, not a slow-way. I'd like to get home before dawn."

"You're out of your mind, Anek. That's the thinner talking."

"Listen, if you won't do it, I'll do it myself," he said, reaching over me for the throttle.

"Fine," I said, brushing his hand away. "I'll do it. Just give me a second."

We slowly gathered speed along the empty highway— thirty-five, forty, forty-five—and after a while, the concrete moving swiftly and steadily below our feet, I was beginning to feel a little more comfortable. Anek put his arms around my waist again, his chin still on my shoulder.

"Good," he whispered into my ear. "Good, good. You've got it. You're fucking doing it. You're really coasting now, boy. Welcome to the third gear, my little man."

"Now," he said. "Try fourth."

I didn't argue this time. I just twisted the accelerator some more, popped the bike into fourth, sliding smoothly off the seat then quickly back on. This time, to my surprise, our course didn't even waver. It was an easy transition. We were cruising comfortably now at sixty, sixty-five, seventy, seventy-five, faster and faster and faster still, the engine singing a high note beneath us as we flew along that straight and empty speedway. We didn't say a word to each other the rest of the way. And nothing seemed lovelier to me than that hot wind howling in my ears, the night blurring around us, the smell of the engine furiously burning gasoline.

DRAFT DAY

On a pleasant morning in April I go three doors down to Wichu's house and we walk to Wat Krathum Sua Pla, the temple where the annual district draft lottery will be held. Wichu has been my best friend all my life. It is hardly sunup, the air thick and cool with dew. We walk silently through our neighborhood. The teashops. The dilapidated playground. The pond with its perpetual scrim of scum. The mangy strays sleeping haphazardly in the streets. The elderly Chinese women gossiping and exercising by the Shinto shrine. The porridge and plantain vendors. The Burmese refugees unloading thick bundles of *Thai Rath* and *Matichon* for the newsstand. We walk silently past all that we know like we know our own skins, all that we will remember fondly in our separate ways, though we regard them then as impediments to our youthful, inchoate ambitions. This is a few years before the neighborhood started sinking into the marsh ground upon which it had been built. This is before the floods got worse with every monsoon and the river rats appeared by the thousands and you could hear them plashing and squealing at night. Before those who could afford it fled for higher ground, my mother and my father included among them.

Wichu and I had been drinking the night before at a small bar in the fresh market. Cane liquor hot in our veins, we'd promised to pray for one another. We weren't religious—the last time we'd been to temple was to admire the swimsuits at the Miss Jasmine Pageant—but we agreed to pray just in case the gods decided to interest themselves in the Pravet District draft lottery. It couldn't hurt, we decided. We drank one last dram to seal the agreement, then we went home.

What Wichu didn't know then was that he needed my prayers more than I needed his. But I didn't tell him that. I didn't tell him everything had already been arranged for me. I didn't tell him that my father's boss's older brother—a retired navy lieutenant—had recently received two crates of Johnny Walker Blue and a certificate for his wife to a famous goldsmith in Pomprapsattruphai District. I didn't tell Wichu that the lieutenant, in turn, had called my father to thank him. He told my father that he'd recommended me to the draft board as an upstanding young citizen, so upstanding I didn't need the benefits of marching drills and mess hall duty and combat training to improve my character in any way. I was a fully formed patriot, he'd told the draft board. A resplendent example for the nation's youth. A true son of Siam. Which means there's nothing to worry about, the lieutenant told my father. Everything has been arranged. Just have your son show up at the lottery.

This was the first and only secret I would keep from Wichu. I prayed for him when I got home from the bar, just as I'd promised. I prayed as I hadn't prayed since I was a child. I don't know if Wichu prayed for me, too, but as I lay in bed waiting for sleep I hoped that he'd save all his prayers for himself.

The next morning I arrive at Wichu's house at the appointed hour. His mother fusses with his hair and his cuffs at the front door. She's wearing a phathung pulled over her breasts, her shoulders caked with menthol powder, her hair wet and jet-black from her morning bath. Wichu wears the outfit she bought specifically for the occasion: a neatly pressed white button-down; crisp, black polyester slacks; a new pair of brown Bata loafers, buffed bright with Kiwi shoe polish. She's even borrowed a gold watch from a friend who hawks them to farangs on Soi Cowboy; it hangs loosely from Wichu's wrist like a bangle, glinting in the weak morning light. She believes that the less Wichu looks like a day-laborer's son—something he'd in fact been until the day-laborer died before Wichu could commit him to memory—the less the draft board will be inclined to put a red ticket in his hand when he reaches into the lottery urn. A red ticket means losing her youngest son to two years of duty, just as she lost her eldest, Khamron, who'd been drafted though he drank a whole bottle of fish sauce, who arrived at the lottery violently ill, and who came home eighteen months later from the Burmese border with a vacant look in his eyes, a letter of commendation and honorable discharge, and a flower of shrapnel buried in his right leg slowly poisoning his bloodstream.

Wichu's mother eyes me curiously when I arrive. I'm wearing tattered blue jeans, a white T-shirt, rubber slippers. I haven't showered. I haven't even brushed my teeth. For a moment, I am afraid she will say something, ask about my relaxed appearance. I am afraid she has found me out and will wonder aloud to Wichu. So I look at Wichu instead. He's clearly hungover, embarrassed by his mother's fussing.

Ma, he says. We'll be late.

She relents, puts her hands in her lap and looks at them sheepishly, as if afraid they'll spring to life again on their own. Wichu leans down and kisses his mother on the cheek.

Gotta go, he says. See you later, Ma.

His mother kisses him back. And then she kisses me. She is a small woman; she has to grab my forearm, pull me down to her, and teeter on her toes just to peck me on the cheek. This is not the first time she has kissed me as she has kissed her own sons. Years later I will remember her kiss on that draft day morning, the scent of menthol wafting from her shoulders, the way her wet hair sprinkled my cheek, and I will feel like I'm falling from some great and excruciating height and the feeling will refuse to leave me for days.

You two take care of each other now, she says. I'm taking a half-day, Wichu, so I'll be along to the temple by noon. Don't pick without me, you hear? Wait until I get there. Tell them you want your mother there to witness it. Think *black*, Wichu. That's what we want. Black, black, black, black, black.

And then she goes back inside the house, as if she cannot bear to watch us leave. My own parents, in the meantime, are sleeping soundly in their beds, three houses away.

When Wichu and I arrive at the temple, there's a crowd of boys lined up inside the open-air pavilion. I'd never seen so many boys be so silent together. We join them there, seat ourselves at the end of the snaking line. Sparrows skitter in the rafters. The ceiling fans whir above us. A few boys eye us silently before turning their attention back to the stage at the front of the pavilion, where military personnel walk back and forth like stagehands preparing for a play. A banner hangs over the stage in the requisite tricolor: PRAVET DISTRICT DRAFT LOTTERY, it announces in bold script. FOR NATION. FOR RELIGION. FOR MONARCHY. Wichu asks me if I'm nervous. I tell him that I am. Wichu says he's not nervous at all. It's strange, he says, I'm feeling calm right now. Relaxed. What will happen will happen.

The pavilion has been roped off. Relatives station themselves along the ropes on straw mats and blankets, waving and smiling to their sons, their nephews, their boyfriends, their grandsons, their fathers in some cases. They fan themselves with the day's paper, eat and drink out of tin canteens. Most of the boys do not acknowledge them, though a few send back weak, assuring smiles. Here and there, men in fatigues walk along the lines, ask the boys questions and jot down notes onto their clipboards. Soft upcountry music has been piped into the pavilion. Wichu taps his fingers absentmindedly to the rhythm. He wants to be a drummer. We've been planning to start a rock 'n' roll band.

When eight o'clock arrives we all stand up and sing the national anthem, followed by the king's. A monk leads us in prayer. Some of the boys murmur the words. Others furrow their brows intently, close their eyes, and chant loudly along with the monk's drone, as if the volume of their prayers this morning might matter a great deal. Wichu and I clasp our hands and stare blankly ahead; we've already prayed the night before. Afterward, there's a loud and nervous silence. A middle-aged man in a uniform darker than the others, dozens of colorful insignias pinned to his shoulders and his breast pockets, walks up to the podium. He looks over us as one looks at one's prized possessions. He's a four-star general, a promotion away from field marshal. We've all seen him on television. He talks into the static-ridden microphone about duty, security, sacrifice, the glory of our great nation, the monarchy's uncompromising integrity, the freedom we all take for granted. Some of the relatives clap during his speech. Some cheer loudly. Most of us just stare. The papers say the general plans to run for a seat in parliament next year; he waves to the relatives when his speech is over, as if practicing the part, bows to the other military personnel onstage. A younger man walks up to the podium when the general leaves. He informs us that registration will now begin.

There are hundreds of us, perhaps even a thousand. The sun has risen high above the mango grove at the edge of the temple when Wichu and I finally get to the registration table. There, a young woman in a tight-fitting military uniform asks us questions. We produce the required documents for her: birth certificates, proofs of residency, identification cards, driver's licenses. Wichu's mother has prepared a whole dossier of other documents and he hands the folder to the woman now: elementary school report cards, doctors' notes about his asthma, letters of recommendation from the owners of the houses she cleans, Khamron's honorable discharge, even his father's certificate of death from the hospital. Wichu's mother believes that—if given to the right person—these documents might send Wichu home. I notice Wichu shaking imperceptibly when he hands over the folder. The woman looks over the documents, flipping through them quickly. When she's done, she looks at Wichu like he's diseased. What is this? she asks impatiently. Wichu shrugs. The woman hands the folder back to him. She tells us both to seat ourselves at the end of another line for the physical exam.

We wait a couple more hours in the physical examination line. The pavilion air has become unbearably hot. More relatives arrive, station themselves by the ropes; it is as if they've come together for a picnic or a boxing match. Wichu seems shaken by the encounter with the woman. I try to make small talk, but he just nods and smiles at me demurely.

The boys line up eight at a time at the front of the line. They take off their shirts for the doctors on duty. They look at their feet while the doctors put cold stethoscopes to their chests, examine their ears, teeth, nostrils, check for scoliosis, measure their height, weight, wingspan, waist, chest—their bodies reduced to so many numbers. The doctors' assistants take notes on their clipboards. Some of the waiting boys jeer and laugh when the fat kids take off their shirts.

Every so often, a doctor gestures to one of the men in fatigues and a boy is told to put on his shirt and go home. When this happens, there is always a bright burst of cheering and clapping among some of the relatives.

A kratoey with heavy makeup wearing a red blouse arrives at the front of the line. When he takes off his blouse, everybody—all the boys waiting in line and all the relatives behind the ropes—laugh and clap and point, even the officers watching from the stage. The kratoey smiles defiantly, his painted face strange on his dark, skinny torso, before bowing to the crowd flamboyantly. I recognize him. The kratoey is a boy named Kitty that Wichu and I knew in high school. Although it is well-known that some boys will arrive at the lottery in drag to try to evade the process, Kitty is not a draft day kratoey. When Kitty passes the physical exam and gets sent to the next line, there is laughter and applause again, and Kitty blows kisses at us all. When the commotion dies down, I hear a boy sitting in front of us say to his friend that we're all fucked now if that kratoey can pass his physical. The friend grunts and tells the story of his uncle, who had chopped off the tip of his pinky finger to avoid the draft thirty years ago.

He cut it off, the boy says. And they drafted him anyway. Told him he didn't need a pinky to pull a trigger.

Wichu and I finally arrive at the front of the line. I wonder if I will be sent home now, if this is what the navy lieutenant meant when he told my father that everything would be arranged. But the doctor examines me like all the other boys. We get sent to the next line, take our seats before the stage. We watch the woman who'd registered us set up the lottery urn. We sit and wait for the rest of the boys to be examined. It's early afternoon now. The doctors pack up their bags, bid the officers good-bye. A man walks to the podium. We're to take an hour break for lunch before the lottery begins.

Wichu's mother has arrived. She gestures to Wichu. Wichu walks over to her. She's wearing her housecleaning uniform. She waves at me, smiles, and I return the courtesy. I watch Wichu kiss her on the cheek, watch her fuss over his hair and his shirt again. She's brought us lunch, and Wichu carries the canteen back to our seats. As we eat, Wichu asks me if my parents are coming. I tell him no. I tell him that my parents are too nervous; I tell him they can't bear to watch. The truth, of course, is that my parents have gone to Chatuchak to buy birds-of-paradise for my mother's garden. Wichu nods. The lunch his mother has prepared—pork fried rice and green eggplant curry—tastes bitter and metallic in my mouth. But I am famished and devour it anyway. All the other boys are eating as well. Soon, the air is a potent admixture of home-cooked dishes. The sparrows in the rafters flutter down to peck at food spilled on the pavilion floor.

After we finish eating, Wichu and I share a jasmine tea. As I'm taking a swig, an officer—a balding, middle-aged man with a gut like a melon and a toothpick between his teeth— taps me on the shoulder. He smells strongly of whiskey and nicotine and cologne. A dark map of sweat soaks his shirtfront.

He asks me if I am who I am. I nod. He asks me to come with him. Wichu looks panicked. He asks the officer if there's a problem, but the officer just adjusts his toothpick, moves it to the other side of his mouth, and says:

No problem, son. Nothing to worry about. Your friend's in good hands.

I do not look at Wichu as the officer talks. When I get up to follow the officer, Wichu taps me on the forearm. He smiles and asks me if I'll be okay. I pause for a moment, standing, peering down into my friend's face, not quite understanding his question.

I realize then that Wichu knows. Of course he knows. He was here, at this temple, outside of the pavilion with his mother, when Khamron got drafted years ago. He was here when the wealthier boys got taken out of the line. He was here when those same boys came back an hour later, took their places at the end of the lottery line, and—when their turns came—drew black card after black card after black card. Wichu had told me all about it the night of his brother's draft. Although I had only half listened to him at the time, the memory of his voice comes back to me now in all its anger.

Hey, he says again, still smiling. You gonna be okay?

I understand then that he's not really asking about my well-being. He's asking for penitence. He's asking for an explanation. He's asking me why I didn't tell him beforehand. The officer clears his throat impatiently beside me. I muster a smile, though I feel nauseated. I tell Wichu to save me my place in line.

I follow the officer out of the pavilion, across the temple grounds toward the monks' quarters. I walk head down, try not to look at the relatives when I walk past, though I feel all their eyes on my back. The officer offers me a cigarette. Though I desperately want one I tell him that I do not smoke. When we arrive at the monks' quarters, there's a small crowd of boys sitting there, smiling and laughing and talking exuberantly. I take my place among them. Years later I will wonder if I could've said something to the officer, told him Wichu's name. But that draft day morning I just sit down on the teakwood floor, filled with relief even as I feel dizzy with dread, thinking of Wichu's smiling face, of him asking me, his voice a frightening monotone, if I was going to be okay.

The lottery begins. All the boys in the monks' quarters fall silent. We listen to a booming voice in the pavilion announce each boy's name one by one over the speakers, followed by the color of the ticket drawn. *Sorachai Srijamnong: Red. Kawin Buasap: Red. Surin Na Nakhon: Black. Worawut Chaiyaprasoet: Red.* The crowd is silent with every red, uproarious with each black. I listen for Wichu's name. I look at the other boys; I wonder if they, too, are listening for their friends' names out in the pavilion.

The officer who escorted me earlier appears. He tells us to go back and seat ourselves at the end of the lottery line. Some of the boys get nervous. They ask him why. This isn't what we'd agreed, says one of the boys. Why don't you send us home already. But the officer tells us not to worry. You pansies, he says, grinning. Relax. Nothing's gonna happen to daddy's little boys.

So we return to the pavilion, walk back single file across the temple ground. When we take our seats at the end of the lottery line, the other boys turn around to look. Word has already spread about us, about the boys who'd been taken out of the line before the end of the lunch hour. I hear relatives on the sidelines hissing and murmuring among themselves.

Fucking corruption, somebody says.

Cowards, says another.

Just another day in the Kingdom of Thailand.

I see the back of Wichu's head some twenty meters ahead, the only thing I recognize in that sea of black and brown before me. He has not turned around to look at our entrance. He's staring into his hands, leaning on his knees.

I see his mother, though. I do not want to meet her eyes, but it is already too late. We look at each other and when we do, I feel my cheeks flush. She nods at me once and then she turns back to look at the boy onstage. She will not look at me again for the rest of the day.

The boy onstage wraps his fingers around the amulet dangling from his neck with one hand, reaches into the lottery urn with the other. *Red*. A moan comes from a section in the crowd. The boy walks off looking stunned, drags his feet across the stage, while the speaker announces another name.

You're all right, boy, a man yells from the sidelines. The boy ignores him. You're all right, the man says again.

The new draftees are being sent to the pagoda, where officers wait for them with scissors and shears. They get their hair cut standing up, small towels draped around their necks like scarves. A few temple novices sweep the piles of hair around their feet. Soon, there's a crowd of young men watching the lottery outside the pavilion shade, their scalps shiny under the afternoon sun. Nice haircut, I hear somebody say to a boy who's been drafted.

Around four, Kitty walks onstage. There's laughing and clapping again, but this time Kitty just fingers the hem of his blouse. *Krittaphong Turapradit*, the speaker system announces, and I realize that I haven't heard Kitty's real name in a very long time. Even from where I am sitting, I can see beads of sweat glistening on Kitty's forehead. I see Wichu sit up straight to watch. Kitty retrieves a handkerchief from his purse to wipe away the sweat. The crowd quiets down while the officer spins the lottery urn; the mechanism's creaking echoes through the pavilion. Kitty reaches into the urn with his eyes shut and pulls out a card. He hands it to the officer. *Black*. The crowd cheers, though there are also a few groans of sadistic disappointment.

Kitty leaps up and down like a jubilant child, his red blouse flapping wildly against his torso. When an officer tries to escort Kitty off the stage, he faints and collapses to the floor, like somebody has reached down and yanked the spine from his back, and there is laughter all around as the officers try to revive him.

The names march on, reds interrupted every so often by a few blacks. It is almost Wichu's turn now. I see his mother chewing her nails to the quick. She waves at Wichu every so often, but Wichu just keeps on staring into his hands.

The boys around me are nervous. I don't get it, one of them says. No way in hell they're making me get up there. Our fathers already gave them what they wanted, right? The other boys tell him to shut up. It'll work out, one of them says. I'm sure they'll send us home soon.

Evening is upon us. The insects are out, moths fluttering against the pavilion lights. Many of the relatives have gone home with their sons to celebrate the miraculous appearance of a black card or, as is more often the case, to prepare their sons for the service in a week's time. There are about a hundred of us left.

Wichu has moved to the front of the line.

The boy before Wichu draws a black card. He gives the finger to all the officers onstage and, in a loud booming voice that surprises us all, tells them to go fuck themselves. His parents and siblings jump up and down at the side of the pavilion, hugging one another, screaming with joy. Wichu's mother is really nervous now. She leans against one of the rope-poles, her right leg jiggling wildly as if possessed, her mouth moving silently. *Wichu Rattanaram*, the speaker system says. Wichu gets up there and looks over the crowd. For a moment, I think he might be looking directly at me. In my head, I am thinking of a prayer. The officer spins the urn. I think I can hear the cards fluttering in there like so many birds. *Black, black, black,* I think. Wichu reaches into the urn, pulls out a card, hands it to the officer. *Red*, the speaker system says, and I can almost see Wichu's shoulders slump from some invisible weight.

I look at Wichu's mother. She is not jiggling her leg any longer, nor is she biting her nails. She merely stares out at Wichu, waves weakly to him. She seems calm. He walks off the stage to get his hair cut at the pagoda, that folder of useless documents still tucked under his arm.

The rest of the evening is like a dream to me now. I don't remember much at all. I only remember Wichu arriving at the side of the pavilion to greet his mother with his head shaved. I only remember his mother reaching out to touch his scalp, to pull his head down into her bosom. He hands her his marching orders and she inspects it for a moment before tucking the document into the folder. The boys who'd been with me in the monks' quarters start to go onstage then, the last of the year's lottery. They pull out black card after black card after black card, like magicians pulling rabbits out of a hat. Nobody cheers for our black cards.

The sun has set, a light evening drizzle singing against the pavilion roof. Most of the relatives have gone home. Wichu's mother, I see, has also gone home. But Wichu stays. He stands there and watches us pull out our black cards from the urn, a blank look on his face, his clean white shirt and crisp new slacks and buffed Bata loafers getting wet in the rain. He never looks at me. I want him to leave. After a while, I can't look at him anymore.

They finally call my name. I walk onstage, though it seems they are calling somebody else. For the first time, that name doesn't sound like my own. So I stand there for a moment before reaching into the urn to receive that generous fate which is mine and mine alone. And when I do, when I hand my black card to the officer and walk off the stage, I look toward the ropes and see that Wichu has finally gone on home without me.

SIGHTSEEING

We're on the southbound train, the tracks swift beneath our feet, the windows rattling in their frames. The train crawls slowly down the archipelago, oceans bordering both sides of the tracks. To the east, the Hunan runoff softens the soil, silt spilling into the ocean, turning the Gulf of Thailand brown. Mountains shield the west from the monsoons, leaving the leeward coast barren and dry, the Andaman Sea retaining its crisp cool blue. We're going through Prachuap Khiri Khan now, where the mountains recede briefly into a flattened plain, the seas pinching the peninsula into a needle. We are going through the slimmest part of the slimmest peninsula in the world, the Indian and the Pacific crashing against both shores. The earth is a tightrope; our train speeds across the flat thin wire. They say that a century from now this will all be gone, that the oceans will rise above this threadbare patch of earth, creating a strait as narrow as Molucca, as fine as Gibraltar, yoking the oceans, severing this nation in two. I can't quite believe this because I never believe anything I won't be around to see.

We're going to Koh Lukmak, the last in a long chain of
Andaman Islands, a tiny fortress of forest and stone. Ma's boss
had a picture of Lukmak on the office bulletin board for years
and Ma said she wanted to see what all the fuss was about.
The fine sand. The turquoise water. The millions of fishes
swimming in the shallow. Her boss had called it paradise, and
though I remember Ma telling me as a child that Thailand was
only a paradise for fools and farangs, for criminals and foreign-
ers, she's willing to give it a chance now. If paradise is really
out there, so close to home, she might as well go and see for
herself.

It is not an easy trip—twelve hours by train, eight hours
by boat—and Lukmak is so small it rarely appears on most
maps. In a few hours, we will step off this train and sleep in
Trang. We will leave that small seaboard town at daybreak,
hire a boat at Tha Tien. The boat will be small and thin.
With the monsoon's approach in a few months' time, our
vessel will skip dangerously along the sea's hard current. We
will stop to rest and take lunch at Koh Trawen, the first of
the Andaman Islands, an abandoned penal colony. We will
leave Trawen after lunch, board the same small boat, get to
Lukmak by nightfall.

Sightseeing, Ma said when we bought our tickets at the
station in Bangkok. We'll be farangs. We'll be just like the
tourists.

This is my last summer with Ma. At the end of the summer, I am to leave for a small vocational college up north.

I watch the blue of the Andaman on the right side of the train. Ma is turned the other way, watching the murky brown of the Gulf. Her window is open. She presses her face against the warm wind, her long black hair whipping wildly around her, the thin navy blue blouse fluttering against her chest. Our shoulders knock every so often, rocking to the motion of the train. We have barely spoken since we left Bangkok early this morning from Hua Lamphong Station.

I break the silence. I tell her to look straight ahead, toward the front of the car. I ask if she can see both oceans out of the corners of her eyes. She smiles and tells me she can. One eye blue, one eye brown. My mother puts a hand on my knee. Then we are silent again, eyes fixed on the front of the car. We know that soon the mountains will rise and we shall be committed to one side of the peninsula—blue or brown; that the sun shall set and the oceans will soon be dark and inhospitable; that the earth only thins and flattens out long enough for us to see two oceans at a single glance; that only a handful of people ever get to see this in their lifetime. Above all, Ma and I know that if things were different, if our lives were simply following their ordinary course, we would never have taken the time to notice such sights.

The beginnings seem so obvious now, though they did not present themselves so clearly to me then. False steps. Spilled coffee. Porcelain cups ratcheting against the kitchen counter.

Cuts and cooking burns, welts white against her dark arm. Bruises on her legs from running into furniture, ebony rosettes blooming on her unblemished skin. Shoulders knocking against doorframes. Her penciled eyebrows more arched than usual, uneven sometimes, the naked flesh of a brow peeking from beneath a thin charcoal line.

But I am at first too busy to give these things much thought. I am too absorbed with the life I plan to lead in the north, on my own, away from Ma. I spend nights in my room studying the vocational college's pamphlets, its maps and course guide, brochures of the nearby town. I familiarize myself with the surrounding geography, dream of the mountains that nestle the campus, of a steady provincial peace away from Bangkok's cacophony—its congestion, its heat, its concrete facades. I make copious lists of the belongings I will take with me. I revise this list endlessly. I pack and unpack into the night hours though my departure is still many months away.

One morning, Ma misjudges the last step coming down the stairs, turns her ankles. She steadies herself with a hand on the banister.

"You all right, Ma?" I laugh. She steadies herself, widens her eyes. She blinks twice. She smooths out her dress with both hands, pulls the strap of her purse back onto her shoulder.

"Oh dear," she says, chuckling. "Don't know what's with me these days. Just a little overworked, I guess. Too many things on my mind."

A few days later, she's not going to work. She's home, reclined on the couch, watching television in her pajamas.

"You sick, Ma?"

"It's just this migraine," she says, holding a hand to the side of her head. A migraine. Migraines never stopped her before. She's a woman who doesn't miss work. Not ever. Not for migraines, not for flus, not for colds. Not for monsoons, not for landslide warnings. Not even for the military's curfew a few years ago, when the Red Cross carried wounded protestors on bloodied stretchers into the lobby of her office building. She's a woman who once went to work with malaria and was asked to go home because her boss found her in the bathroom throwing up. Even then, she insisted on going back to work—until she fainted in the middle of a company meeting. An ambulance had to be called; she went back to work the very next day.

"I'm glad you're taking some time off, Ma. Should I take you to a doctor?"

She smiles at me from the couch, turns back to the television, snuggles up against one of the pillows.

"It's okay. I already took some medicine. Feeling much better already. Go on ahead to school, luk. Don't worry about me."

But two weeks later, there is nothing but worry for both of us. Two weeks later, while I'm downstairs having my breakfast, spooning the last of my rice porridge, I hear a loud crash coming from the upstairs bathroom. I hear the shower trickling, the electric water pump whirring and wheezing in the back of the house, and then there's another loud thudding, the sound of something heavy hitting the ground. I walk to the bottom of the stairs, call up to my mother. I ask if she's okay, but there's just a long unending silence. There's just the slow, steady trickle of the shower.

I'm up the stairs. I'm at the bathroom door.

"You okay, Ma?"

"Sorry. Just dropped something."

There's a weak, sheepish chuckle in her voice and then, as I'm walking back toward the staircase, I hear the sound of skin slipping against porcelain tiles, like a car screeching to a halt. I hear that thudding again, louder this time. It's like the footsteps of giants. Like fists hitting sandbags. Like my mother hitting the bathroom floor.

The door isn't locked. It's as if she knew this would happen, as if she'd left the door unlocked that morning thinking, *Just in case.* I open the bathroom door. I see my mother's silhouette through the shower curtains, a small heap on the floor, thick clouds of steam billowing through the room. I walk toward the shower. I throw the curtains open on my mother's nakedness. I help my mother get up. Her irises roam wildly back and forth across the ceiling. Her small hands reach out for my arms. Her fingernails dig into my flesh. Her mouth opens and closes like a fish out of water, gasping for air.

It is then that the barely noticed details start to fall into place—the clumsiness, the bruises and cuts, the misjudged steps, the misshapen eyebrows, the days off from work. I turn off the shower. I wrap a towel around her small, naked body. I help my mother get up. This is the first time that I have seen my mother naked. I look at the way her breasts sag like up-turned bells, nipples bulbous like baby mangosteens. I look at the thick thatch of hair between her legs. I look at that lost look of shame on her face.

My mother is going blind.

The doctors say her eyes have deteriorated beyond repair. Migraine-induced retinal detachment. They tell us that if she had checked in a couple of months earlier, when the migraines started, when the pain behind her eyes began, blindness might have been averted. They tell us it's too late now. We take the three-hour trip to Bangkok Christian—a private hospital that took care of the prime minister when he lost his right eye in a shooting accident—to get one last opinion.

The ophthalmologist at Bangkok Christian mentions experimental surgery. But he informs us that the success rate has been slim thus far. He says Ma would risk going blind altogether from the procedure. It is something called a "vitrectomy": taking my mother's eyes out of their sockets, soldering the fallen retina back to the vitreous, putting them back in again. The ophthalmologist says the procedure will be very expensive. A surgeon would have to be flown in from Singapore. He says this with a smile. His stiff, white lab coat shimmers under the bright fixtures.

"Money's not an issue, Doctor." I say this curtly, though I know it is a lie. My mother and I have never purchased a plane ticket for ourselves, let alone for some stranger from Singapore. Ma tells the ophthalmologist we'll think it over. We leave Bangkok Christian with nothing new. Four doctors now and still the same old story.

Eight to ten weeks before permanent loss of sight. Retinas detached, vitreous shrunken, optic nerves irrevocably damaged. Stay out of the sun. No bright lights. No small print. Do eye exercises. Focus on slowly moving objects. We need to keep the retinas stimulated, on the off chance they might regenerate. On the off chance. In case of a miracle. Get lots of sleep. Don't go to work. You really can't go to work, ma'am. But above all, don't panic. But most important, please relax.

My mother quits her job. Later that week, we look at a map of Thailand together, tracing the hatchet-shaped boundaries, circling places she would like to see. Lop Buri. Chiang Rai. Loie. Samut Songkhram. Mae Hong Son. The doctors tell Ma to get out of the city, take a vacation. We decide to go to the Andaman Islands.

And in my room that week I unpack my belongings once more. I don't repack them this time. I put all of the books back on the shelf, stack the brand-new notebooks under my desk. I move the course guide, the maps, and the brochures from the head of my bed, stow them away in a drawer. Though I still take them out from time to time, flip through the now-familiar pages, I'm finding it difficult to dream of those mountains again. I cannot look at those maps without imagining my mother blind and alone in the house, and I'm starting to wonder, for the first time in my life, about what kind of son I really am.

The train comes to a stop in Trang. I try to take my mother's arm when we get up.

"I'm not blind yet, luk."

"Sorry, I just thought—"

"You just thought nothing, luk. I'm fine."

The sun is gone, the tree-lined horizon red from the last of its rays. Moths dance against the platform's flickering lamplights. When we step off the train, Ma puts on her sunglasses: horn-rimmed, purple-rhinestoned Armanis we bought at the Chatuchak Bazaar. She wears those sunglasses every chance she gets now. Doctor's orders. They suit her well, and if it wasn't for the fact that sunglasses look out of place in the evenings, I'd say my mother might be a Chinese movie star.

We check into our hotel room, have dinner at a noodle vendor in the center of town. We order large bowls of seafood vermicelli, sit at a small table on the sidewalk. We eat by the weak light of the town's streetlamps.

"You okay?" Ma asks, tugging at the noodles with her chopsticks, peering over her sunglasses, thin wreaths of steam unfurling between us.

"I'm fine. Why?"

"You're not being very talkative, that's all. You've been a little morose. A mother notices, you know."

"Is there something you want to talk about?"

"Oh, I don't know. Something. Anything. Everything. For God's sakes, we're on vacation, luk. Smile a little."

"Fine, let's talk."

"Okay, let's talk."

"Okay." She chews off the head of a prawn, smiling, twirling the translucent husk between her fingers. "Why don't you tell me about the school up north, luk. What do you think you'll study? I don't think we've ever talked about that before."

"I haven't given it much thought, actually."

"No?"

"No, Ma."

"But you were so excited a few months ago."

"That was a few months ago, Ma."

"What did you tell me you were going to study? What was it, luk? Libraries? That was it, wasn't it? Oh, I think you'd make a great librarian. You'd be so handsome with all those books."

"Let's talk about something else, Ma."

There's an awkward silence. Ma puts down her chopsticks. She takes off her sunglasses, folds the thick plastic earpieces, lays them neatly on the table. I can see the faint outline of rings already forming around her eyes. I bend to sip my broth.

"Look at me, luk. No. Look at me."

I put the bowl down, lean back in my seat.

"I didn't bring you along so you could brood. I would've come myself, luk, if I knew you were going to act this way. What's wrong with a little conversation with your mother? I'm not asking for much here, luk. I'm just asking you to be courteous. I'm just asking you to be kind."

"Sorry, Ma. I just didn't—"

"Don't 'sorry' me, luk. I don't need your apologies. I just need you to act like you're my son, that's all—not some cranky client I'm taking out to dinner. Be decent, luk. Be nice. Is that too much to ask?"

"Ma—"

"You think it's easy for me to sit here knowing I'm going blind, that there's nothing I can do about it? I could wake up blind tomorrow morning. I might never see you again. And you'll be sorry then, luk. Real sorry. You'll probably be sorrier than you've ever been in your life, knowing that the last time your mother saw you, you were being dreadful."

We finish our meals silently. On our way back to the hotel, there's a blind man playing an accordion on the corner across from the hotel. He sings a southern worksong, his contralto lilting across the street. Pedestrians drop change in the tin cup at his feet and he smiles at the sound of each brightly clinking coin. For a moment, as we walk past, I wonder where his children are. Then Ma and I look away. From our room three stories up, we can hear him singing all through the night. We sleep to the sounds of his beggar's elegies.

Every Saturday morning, Ma battles the vendors at Chatuchak. Even the most stubborn of vendors have submitted to her entreaties. It is not only charm she exerts upon them, for charm will get you only so far; Ma slashes their prices through an inimitable combination of wit, commonsense economics, high theatrics, and old-fashioned psychological manipulation. That Saturday at the bazaar, a few days before our trip, Ma was at the height of her powers.

The vendor was a young, homely-looking girl. Throngs of people filed past her booth. I stood at a distance as Ma scanned the hundreds of frames neatly laid out on the table. "What do you think?" she asked, putting on the Armanis.

"They look good, Ma."

"Really?"

"Yeah. You look like Jackie Kennedy."

This pleased her. She raised her hand in a fluttering half-gesture, smiling, bending to look at her reflection in the small mirror. "How much?" she finally asked, taking off the glasses with a swift, dramatic gesture. The vendor said twelve hundred. Ma yelped. "They're real, ma'am," the vendor said. "Real Armanis."

"Real or not, that's an awful lot of money."

The girl laughed—a shrill, sheepish sound. A middle-aged Chinese couple walked into the booth, the husband with a vacant look in his eyes. Ma asked for a discount. "I can't, ma'am. Profit margin's small as it is."

"C'mon. Give an old woman a break."

The girl smiled. She said eleven hundred. Ma yelped again.

"I'm not a farang, na? We're all Thai here. Give me the Thai price." The vendor asked Ma to name one. Not eleven hundred, Ma said. The vendor counteroffered: ten-fifty. Ma put the glasses back on the table. "That's ridiculous," she said, shaking her head, though I could hear that hint of mischief in her voice. Only now, I knew, would the bargaining begin in earnest. "Let's go," Ma said curtly, feigning disappointment. The Chinese couple glanced at us, smiled, and I tried to return the courtesy. The wife went back to browsing and the husband to looking as if he would rather be elsewhere. "Can you believe that?" Ma asked as we made our way toward the aisle, her voice loud enough for the girl to hear. "Twelve hundred for a pair of fake Armanis."

"Ma—"

"Don't 'Ma' me. You don't think it's a little expensive?"

"Well—"

"It's outrageous."

There is faith in the way Ma bargains, in the way we started to walk away from the girl. Her faith was substantiated that day. The girl called us back.

"Ma'am! Ma'am!" Ma let go of my arm, turned to face the vendor.

"How's a thousand, ma'am?" the girl said, getting up from her seat.

"Oh no." Ma laughed, grabbing my arm again. "Why would I spend that kind of money on a pair of fake Armanis?" Out of the corner of my eye, I saw the Chinese husband snickering softly to himself.

"They're not fake, ma'am."

"Oh?"

"No, ma'am. My boyfriend got them from the factory."

"So they're stolen?"

"Ma'am!"

"Pirated, then. They're pirated. You know I could—"

"Ma'am!"

"I'm just teasing. What's a little teasing?" Ma said. "Don't take an old woman like me so seriously. Here. Let me look at them again."

Ma tried them on once more. The girl told her she looked stunning. "I like them," Ma said, taking off the glasses. "But a thousand? I don't like them *that* much." Again, the girl asked Ma to name a price. Ma took out her wallet, handed me the sunglasses, fished out a few bills. "Tell you what. I'll leave six hundred baht on this table. Then I'll walk away with those sunglasses."

"Oi! I can't do that, ma'am."

"Of course you can."

"No, ma'am, that's impossible." The girl looked at me. I shrugged. "Okay," Ma said. "Let me ask you this then: How much did you pay for these glasses?"

"I don't know, ma'am. My boyfriend was the one—"

"Oh, just tell me. What's an old woman like me going to do with that kind of information? Your boyfriend's not here now, is he? How else am I supposed to give you a fair offer?"

"I can't do that. I'd lose money if I gave it to you for six hundred, though."

"So six hundred it is then," Ma said emphatically, laying the money down. The Chinese husband let out a bellowing laugh this time and the girl shot him a look that suggested, suddenly, that she was much older than I had originally assumed. "I can't let you do that." The vendor's voice was strong and curt now, a new pallor on her face.

"Now you're talking," Ma teased, smiling. "No need to 'ma'am' me all the time. Now we can talk like adults. How much did you pay for these?" The girl shook her head. Six-fifty, Ma offered. The girl shook her head again. Ma took another hundred-baht note from her wallet. Seven-fifty.

"No."

Ma held the note in her hand, and for a moment they just stood there—the vendor and my mother—locked in a mute battle. I'd seen this type of standoff many times before. I pitied the girl.

"How old are you?" Ma asked suddenly.

"Excuse me?"

"How old are you?"

"I'm twenty-six, ma'am."

"It's a good age to be, twenty-six," Ma said. "You might not think it from the way I look, but it wasn't so long ago when I was your age. It wasn't so long ago at all—though you're far more beautiful than I ever was then."

The girl just blinked at my mother's flattery. The Chinese wife, for the first time, looked our way.

"Here's the situation." Ma put the hundred-baht note on the table with the other bills, patting the pile of money like a bettor blessing her ante. "I'll tell you my problem and then you can decide whether or not to give me those glasses for seven-fifty today. Thing is, those glasses aren't an accessory for me. They're not an optional luxury. You see, I'm going blind. By this time tomorrow, I might not be able to see a thing. Do you understand what I'm saying? You're looking at a woman who's going *blind*. The doctors say those glasses might mean a few more days of sight for me—ask my son if you don't believe me. Now, you don't strike me as the type of girl who'd let a woman go blind over a few hundred bahts. But maybe you are. Maybe you're that type of girl . . ."

"Oh come now, child, have a heart."

It was the Chinese woman, her voice raspy like sandpaper.

Later that day, snaking our way through the aisles of the bazaar, Ma took the bag from my hands, put on the Armanis, and laughed a wild laugh of triumph, turning heads in the hot market.

I wake to the sounds of birds. The beggar has left his corner. Ma is already up, smoking a cigarette on the patio, warm wind rushing through the screen door, her small silhouette dark against the sky's red and yellow hues. She's wearing her sunglasses. When I approach, she flicks the cigarette over the railing.

She's taken to smoking lately, something she's never done before, a pack of Benson & Hedges a day. It's one of many things that make my mother seem a stranger to me now. The sunglasses. The smoking. Ma and I, for the first time, taking a vacation together. The case of Tsingtao beer we've lugged down here with us from Bangkok. My mother drinking beer at all. She wears jeans and blouses and baggy T-shirts instead of neatly tailored business suits. She's stopped wearing makeup as well, and—without the rouged cheeks, the crimson lips, the penciled eyebrows—I sometimes feel like I am seeing my mother's face for the very first time. And I have woken up many times now to Ma sitting at a distance, watching me sleep.

"How long have you been up?" I ask groggily, sinking into the chair next to hers.

"A while. Just wanted to see the sunrise."

"Feeling okay?"

"Fine," she says. "It's better this morning. No black dot yet."

A few days ago, she told me that when her vision faltered, it was like looking through a kaleidoscope. A cold white flash flooded her eyes, and when her eyes refocused, it was like the world was breaking into a million tiny pieces. She had to shut her eyes for a while before the shattered world rearranged itself—before pieces of brown became a chair, pieces of red became a shirt, pieces of cream became her own reflection in the bathroom mirror. Sometimes, when she opened her eyes, the world would still be murky, blurred, like opening her eyes underwater, and it often took a while before things came back into focus again. These spells were getting longer and longer now, but she said she didn't really mind them so long as they went away. What she did mind, however, was what she calls "the black dot": a small black pinprick that begins in the center of her vision and expands in an ever-widening circle, like a dark flower whose blooming slowly smothers her sight. It grows larger and larger every day, and when this happens, Ma has to blink hard to keep the dot at bay.

We watch the sun rise together, the fiery orange slowly peeking over the sea, the first of the Andaman Islands a ghostly shadow on the horizon. Ma gets up from her chair. "I'm going to miss this," she says.

The sea is a sheet of blue. We arrive at the port in Trang, buy our tickets to Koh Lukmak, sit down for a bowl of fish soup.

We have a long journey ahead of us—eight hours at sea. The stench of fish is in the air and, in the distance, ships bob on the horizon in a line, as if strung together by some invisible thread. Gulls swoop down upon docked junkers, pecking at fish guts left to waste on the plywood decks, squawking in their loud, discordant tones.

When we board, Ma promptly falls asleep, lying down across the narrow bench, a lifejacket as a pillow beneath her head, the sun a soft blue glow through the tarpaulin. The boat is long and thin, a sixteen-seater manned by a boy my age. He sits at the stern with the rod of the motor in hand, the blades behind him gurgling beneath the sea's surface, the wind blowing through his reddish, sun-soaked hair. The sun climbs the sky. Waves gently slap against the boat's wooden hull. A couple of farangs sit at the bow, outside of the tarpaulin shade, two white men in gaudy batik shirts passing a thin flask of Mekong whiskey between them. Koh Trawen—the island where we will drop off the farangs and stop for lunch before going on to Lukmak—is a faint hazy specter in the distance.

Before she fell asleep, Ma told me that during the 1930s and '40s, Trawen was a penal colony, a place where the government sent con men, Royalists, dissident writers, and communists. After the war, the prisoners rebelled, murdering all of the authorities on the island. As retribution, the government cut off their rations and left the prisoners there to die, with no means of transport back to the mainland, surrounding the island with a naval patrol so the chaolay—the sea gypsies—could not come to their rescue. The government claimed they all died there after a few years, starved to death on the edge of the maritime border, but there are fishermen who swear that they still see fires in the hills at night, tiny orange flames flickering out across the open sea, the rebels— or perhaps their children; or perhaps their ghosts—waiting to return to the mainland, preparing for their next assault against the military government.

I watch Trawen's faint outline on the horizon. One of the farangs lies down against the bow, his feet resting on the first bench, a cap pulled over his eyes. His friend stashes the whiskey flask into a backpack and smiles at me. I nod. Then he joins his friend on the bow, face up to the sky, draping a towel across his face. The tarpaulin beats overhead like a light sail. Soon, I am the only person awake except for the boy at the stern directing our small boat out into the Indian Ocean. I watch Ma sleeping for a while, watch the rise and fall of her chest. Every time she sleeps, I wonder if she will wake up blind, and I wonder what I'll do then, what we'll say to each other when the time comes. But soon I, too, start to feel drowsy, the small boat rocking like a cradle on the open sea.

When I wake up, Ma is hunched over, her head in her hands.

"Are you okay?" I ask, trying not to panic, though I'm thinking, *It's happened, it's happened. She's blind now.*

"I think I'm seasick, luk. I'm not used to being on boats." I reach under my seat, hand her a bottle of water. "Here," I say. "Drink up. Breathe deep. Don't look at the floor. I hear it helps if you keep your eyes on the horizon."

Ma sits up straight, takes a couple of deep breaths. She sips from the water bottle. Her face is flushed, beads of sweat clinging to her brow. Trawen is larger now—I can almost make out the shape of trees—and I realize that what I had perceived, from a distance, to be one large island is actually a series of them, four or five smaller islands rising around a larger mound. They seem a thousand shades of green now, the colors multiplying with the closing distance.

"Do you need to vomit, Ma?"

Ma shakes her head from side to side, a hand over her mouth. "We're almost there," I say. Ma lets out a groan. "How many more hours from Trawen to Lukmak?" she asks.

"Five, Ma."

"Maybe we should stay at Trawen for the night then, luk. I don't think I can get on this boat again today."

Then Ma is on her knees, her head hanging over the side of the boat, retching and heaving and vomiting. Long streams of light liquid splash into the blue-green surf. I sit on the bench beside her, pull her hair from her forehead, stroke her back. I feel her body tense and relax, tense and relax beneath my hand. She vomits until she cannot vomit any longer, as the farangs look over occasionally before quickly looking away.

"It's best to get it out, madam," the boy says from behind us, his voice carrying over the sputtering engine. From the tone of his voice—easy, matter-of-fact—I can tell that he has tended to many a seasick middle-aged lady. "Just hang on, madam. Trawen won't be long now."

Ma's body relaxes. She reaches down into the surf, scoops up a few mouthfuls of water, spits it back into the ocean. She wipes her mouth with one arm, rests on her elbows against the side of the boat. "You okay, Ma?" She nods quickly, not looking at me, trying to catch her breath. And then Ma widens her eyes, blinks twice. Widens her eyes, blinks twice. Widens her eyes, blinks twice again. She blinks twice, she blinks three times. She reaches out with one hand and grips my thigh tightly, her fingers pinching the skin. I stifle the impulse to yell. I rest a light hand on hers. I urge her on. Widens her eyes, blinks twice. Widens her eyes, blinks twice. Finally, she relaxes her grip and I can feel the blood rushing back to the skin of my thigh. She puts both of her hands in her lap, takes a few deep breaths, and gets up to sit on the seat beside me. "Look at me, luk," she says, her voice weak and frail. "Oh, just look at the state I'm in."

Her hands pat the breast pocket of her blouse, move wildly over her heart. Her eyes dart across the boat's watery bottom.

"What is it, Ma?"

Ma's lips are quivering. Ma's teeth are biting down on the trembling, whitening flesh.

"My—My—Where are—My sunglasses, luk—"

And I imagine the sunglasses slowly falling, the horn-rims and purple rhinestones and the word ARMANI in tiny gold letters spiraling down the blue-green abyss, searching for a resting place on the soft and sandy seafloor.

We decide on a bungalow on the west side of Trawen, a small crescent beach far away from the farangs. With the approaching monsoon, only two of the six bungalows on the beach are occupied. One of the smaller islands around Trawen is but a few hundred meters away, directly facing our bungalow, a modest mound no larger than a city block rising out of the ocean. Earlier, when I asked the boy on the boat if the island had a name, he told me it didn't, it was too small to warrant one. Ma rented one of the bungalows for the boy so he could take us out to Lukmak in the morning and he tied the small boat to one of the pier's barnacle-crusted posts.

Ma falls asleep again after we unpack our bags on the wicker floor, her body splayed across the mattress. I change into my trunks and decide to go for a swim, gently closing the screen door behind me.

The water is as warm as the evening air. I walk out a short distance, my knees slicing through the calm surface. Though we are not at Lukmak yet, it is as Ma hoped it would be: the water like a clear skin stretched over the earth; the sand fine and white and soft as a pillow; the schools of tiny rainbow fishes moving in quick unison. Windcrabs scuttle across the floor, burrowing themselves, leaving fresh divots in the sand.

When the water is up to my waist, I plunge beneath the surface, doing quick breaststrokes away from the beach. My chest skims across the soft, sandy bottom. I come back up for air, take a deep breath, plunge down again. I do it once more, the bottom deeper this time. I can feel the soft incline dip a little more, sense the surface slowly rising above me with every stroke I make along the bottom of the sea. I push up off the bottom with my hands, come up for air, plunge back down again.

I open my eyes this time as I rush to the bottom, kicking hard against the surface. I see soft shafts of sunlight slicing through a thick, bleary haze. Clusters of blue, clusters of yellow, clusters of green disperse all around me, moving as if suspended midair, little pellets of color swimming through a depthless tapestry of light. I hear my feet kicking, my heart beating, the warm water rushing around me. An indistinct seafloor rises up to meet me. I crash into the sand. Perhaps, I think, this is what Ma must feel in the grips of her oncoming blindness. These indistinct visions. These fragmented hues. This weightlessness.

I come back up for air. When I break the surface, I look back onto shore, eyes stinging, lips parched and dry. The bungalow looks small with the island rising up behind it, the sun a golden crown around its peak, the beach a thin white slit in the distance.

I see a door opening, a woman sitting down on the bungalow stairs. She's a red and black dot resting back on her elbows, her feet in the sand. I raise my hand up out of the water to wave to my mother. I'm hoping my mother can see me. I want to believe that she's waving back, that the red and black flutter is the sign of a mother waving to her son. It's me, Ma. Me. I'm swimming back to shore.

The island's electricity generator cuts off with a loud crash at eight. Ma goes inside to fetch the oil lantern, comes back out to sit with me on the beach. The tide has peaked and is beginning to recede.

"Feeling better, Ma?"

"I'm a different person, luk. Sorry about this afternoon."

"Don't be silly, Ma," I say, stretching my legs out in the warm sand. "I'm sorry about the sunglasses."

"Oh," she says, chuckling, lighting a cigarette, fingering the neck of her Tsingtao beer, "they were just silly little things anyway. Probably retribution for taking advantage of that poor girl at Chatuchak."

We sit there silently for a while, listening to the breeze rustling the coconut trees, the waves lapping against the beach, watching the fast shadows of windcrabs racing sideways across the sand.

"Can I ask you a question, luk?"

"Sure."

"Are you going up north at the end of the summer?"

"Well," I say. "Honestly, Ma?"

"Of course."

"I don't know, Ma."

"I was afraid you'd say that."

She takes a drag off her cigarette, the ember casting a soft red glow on her face. She stares out into the darkening ocean. She stubs the cigarette against the beer bottle, sparks flying off the glass.

"Listen to me, luk. Listen to me very carefully." She reaches over and cups my cheeks with her hands. Her palms are cool from the beer. Her touch startles me. "You're going up north at the end of the summer. I don't care what you think—you're going to college. It's what I want for you. You have to go. I don't want you taking care of me, hanging around. I don't expect you to, if that's what you've been worried about all this time. Don't worry. I can take care of myself."

"But Ma—"

"Just listen to me. It's enough that I'm going blind, luk. I don't want you to suffer too. Besides." She takes her hands away, tilts the beer against her lips. "I'm not dying here, luk. I'm just going blind. Just remember that. There's a big difference—a whole world of difference—even if both of those things happen to good people every day."

I wake up to the dark, to the sound of the screen door swinging on its hinges. Ma's sheets are neatly folded on the mattress beside me. I get up, put on a shirt, walk outside, down the bungalow steps. It's quiet save for the wind whistling through the trees, dark except for a flickering flame, bright and orange, throbbing in the distance, moving across the surface of the sea.

I think of the spirit of dead prisoners, of fishermen's tales, but realize quickly that it's only Ma with the oil lantern, that the tide has receded considerably since I went to sleep, the edge of the beach where the water meets the sand some distance away.

The flame of the oil lantern gets smaller and smaller and soon it is merely a pinprick against the dark night. *It's my mother walking on water*, I think. It moves sideways now, moves along the bottom of the dark shadow across the bay, comes to a resting place. *It's my mother on an island with no name.*

I walk toward the water, toward the flickering light. The flame is like an orange eye winking at me from across the divide. The sand is damp, soft as a slab of fresh clay, my feet sinking into its warmth as I walk.

When I come upon the water's edge, I realize there is still considerable distance between where I am standing and the light of Ma's lantern on the island across the bay. Perhaps the water is shallow enough to walk across, but I remember from swimming here yesterday that the bottom quickly falls away and that my mother is not a very strong swimmer.

And then I see it. I see a thin luminous line out of the corner of my eye. I see a thread running faintly across the bay. An opaque sandbar stretched between the islands like an exposed vein.

I walk toward the sandbar, across the beach, my eyes fixed on the flame. I see that the path is no more than a meter wide, a white trail running across the surface of the water. The black sky turns a deep indigo, night slowly relenting to day, and I can make out Ma's small shape sitting beside the flickering lantern. I'm walking onto the sandbar, warm waves licking up across my bare feet, out to watch the sun rise with Ma, and then to bring her back before the tide heaves, before the ocean rises, before this sand becomes the seafloor again.

PRISCILLA THE CAMBODIAN

The only thing I ever learned about wealth was Priscilla the Cambodian's beautiful teeth. All her teeth were lovely ingots, each one crowned in a cap of pure gold. When she smiled it sometimes looked like that little girl had swallowed the sun. Dong and I would often ask to look and Priscilla would open her mouth wide. We'd move in close, stare into its recesses until her jaw got sore. "You're rich," Dong and I would say, and Priscilla the Cambodian would smile and giggle like we'd just told her she was beautiful.

Her father was a dentist. When things started looking bad in Cambodia, he hired somebody to smelt the family's gold. He put all that gold in Priscilla's mouth. And then they took him away. Priscilla remembered sitting on his dentist's chair in the empty hospital while bombs fell on Phnom Penh. Over the next three years, as Priscilla and her mother moved from camp to camp, she sometimes went for days without opening her mouth—her mother was afraid the guards might get ideas. She made Priscilla nibble on gruel and salted fish in the relative secrecy of the warehouse they shared with hundreds of other refugees. "Awesome," we'd say. "They should make a movie about your life, girlie."

This was the summer Dong and I wasted in the empty community pool the development company never got around to finishing. Priscilla and her mother had recently arrived in Bangkok with two other Cambodian families. They all squatted in a tin shack compound by the train tracks bordering the development. Before we met Priscilla, Dong and I in our unflappable boredom would sometimes stand on the rails and throw rocks just to hear the satisfying clang on the Cambodians' corrugated roofs. Priscilla's short, flat-faced mother would run out and bark at us in a language we didn't understand, but it wasn't too hard to understand the rusted shovel she waved threateningly in our direction, so we'd run and laugh like delighted hyenas.

Mother said the refugees were a bad sign. "God's trying to tell us something," she said. "God's probably saying, 'Hey, sorry, but there won't be a health club or a community garden or a playground or a pool or any of those other things you suckers thought you were getting when you first came to the development. I'm gonna give you some Cambodian refugees instead. They're not as fun, but hey, life isn't a store, sometimes you don't get what you pay for.'" Father nodded and said refugees meant one thing and one thing only. It meant we'd be living in the middle of a slum soon. "Those fuckers move in packs," he said. Their little refugee camp would get so big we'd probably start thinking we were refugees too.

By that time the prognosis was already bad. The factories had moved to the Philippines and Malaysia. Mother was reduced to sewing panty hose out of a Chinese woman's house. Father carried concrete beams at a construction site for minimum wage. Some of the families in the development had already moved on, leaving their pets and potted plants and empty duplexes behind. Early in the summer, Father and Mother tried to sell like the others. But the market had turned; it was already too late. When the development company realtor came to appraise, Father's face turned so pale I was afraid he'd pass out. "That's a goddamn crime," Father said, after the realtor offered little more than half the duplex's original price. "No crime here," the realtor replied, fingering the knot of his tie. "Just old-fashioned economics." So Father said, "Get out of my house. Get out or I'm gonna show you something else that's old-fashioned." But the realtor just kept smiling and said, "Fine. Suit yourself. Have fun living like savages."

One April afternoon, Dong and I were breaking our asses attempting stupid bike tricks in the unfinished pool. I sat in the shallow end wiping a stain on my pants while Dong prepared to ride off the diving board. It was going to be a good trick, we thought. A girl-seducing trick. We were sure that once all the girls saw us soar off that diving board and land in the deep end they'd swoon, fall on their knees, and trip over each other in the hopes of doing some delightfully nasty dancing with us. Dong and I had decided that our access to dancing of any kind would not easily be granted on our good looks alone. For one, we were both too dark. For another, my dogged asthma had earned me the moniker of Black Wheezy from the Thicknecks at school. And, for yet another, Dong was knock-kneed and kind of fat. The Thicknecks called him the Pregnant Duck. When girls were around, all they'd have to say was "Hey look, guys, there goes Black Wheezy and the Pregnant Duck" or "Quack-Quack! Hack-hack!" and suddenly it was like the word HANDSOME had just been emblazoned on their foreheads. Needless to say, this was not funny to us at all—not even a little bit—but apparently very funny to Dong's parents and my own, because they laughed so long and hard when we went crying to them that we believed we'd become the most psychotically depressed eleven-year-old boys in the history of the planet. So we needed a talent. Aerial acrobatics seemed like a good idea. Unfortunately, none of our attempts thus far had been very acrobatic or even very aerial.

That afternoon, just as Dong got halfway down the diving board, Priscilla the Cambodian appeared poolside out of nowhere. "Wheeeeee!" she squealed like a happy little succubus. Dong hesitated, turned to look at Priscilla, lost crucial velocity, and tumbled off the edge of the diving board. It made a bad sound. It sounded like a dog getting hit by a car because even with all the bike's clanging and screeching I could still hear Dong yelp when he hit the pool's hard bottom. Priscilla pointed and laughed, and that's when I glimpsed her gold fangs glinting for the very first time.

"Refugee fuckass," Dong muttered, getting up off the mildewed tiles. "What do you think you're doing?" He collected his bike, teetered on his feet. But Priscilla the Cambodian just laughed and laughed some more. "Hey," I said, walking down toward Dong in the deep end. "The pool's ours. Get out of here." She looked at me curiously. She was younger than us. She wore an old Kasikon Bank T-shirt that came down to her knees. Short black hair sprouted in matted tufts all over her head. And she had that mouthful of gold.

She stopped laughing, frowned, pointed an accusing finger at us both. "Leave my mother alone," she said sternly in Thai, her tiny voice echoing around the pool. "No more rocks." Dong and I exchanged glances. We didn't know she could speak Thai. We'd seen her around the housing development with the other Cambodians, but they'd always spoken to each other in that gibberish.

"I don't know what you're talking about," Dong said, rubbing his head with the heel of his palm.

"Don't lie," she answered. I glimpsed her teeth again. I thought about pirates. "I'll kill you next time. I'm not kidding, guys."

"Okay," Dong said, shrugging, getting on his bike. He started riding in large swooping circles, the chain creaking noisily, the wheels singing beneath him. "Sure. Whatever, girlie." She stared at us impassively, watched Dong gliding along the bottom of the pool. "You speak pretty good Thai," I said after a while. "What's your name?"

Dong shot me an incredulous look from his bike.

"Priscilla," she said almost sheepishly, fingering the hem of her T-shirt.

"Some name for a refugee," I replied, laughing. "That's not a Cambodian name. That's a farang name."

She opened her mouth as if she might explain. But then she turned around and started walking away. "Just don't do it again," she said as she went through the unpainted gate. "No more rocks. My mama doesn't like it."

She'd been gone for all of ten minutes when Dong and I climbed up the pool ladder, fished the bike out, and started making our way toward the railroad tracks.

"Did you see her teeth?"

"Yeah," Dong said. "She's a freak."

A thin strand of smoke curled out of Priscilla's shack. Somebody was cooking inside. We stood on the railroad ties, grabbed a few choice rocks, felt their cold, lovely heft in our hands. "Bombs away," Dong said, winking.

The first rock elicited no response. But as soon as the second one rang the corrugated roof, Priscilla emerged from the house like an angry little boar, fists at her sides, nostrils flared, bushwhacking her way through the knoll separating the train tracks from the Cambodians' shanty. I saw her contorted face, started laughing, started sprinting. But halfway back to the road, I noticed Dong wasn't running beside me.

I turned around. That tiny Cambodian girl had Dong pinned facedown to the railroad ties. She sat on his back while he bucked and thrashed beneath her like a rodeo horse. She yelled at him, pummeled the back of his head repeatedly with her hands. I thought about leaving him there. But then I remembered that the girl had said she was going to kill us, and I suddenly didn't know how serious Cambodians were when they said something like that, even if the Cambodian was just a little girl. She could've been Khmer Rouge—a term Mother and Father always mentioned in stern voices when they complained about the refugees—although I only understood at the time that Khmer Rouge was a bad thing like cancer was a bad thing. Khmer Rouge probably made you bald and pale and impossibly skinny, and Khmer Rouge probably made you cough up vile gray-green globs of shit like Uncle Sutichai when we visited him at the hospital every Sunday. If that little girl had Khmer Rouge, I certainly didn't want Dong to get it too.

Dong looked at me helplessly when I arrived. Priscilla had both his arms pinned to the earth with her feet. "Dude," he pleaded. "Do something."

"Say you're sorry!" Priscilla screamed. Dong grunted, struggled some more in vain. She didn't notice I was there. "Say you're sorry!" she screamed again, hitting Dong's head a few more times, the sound flat and dull.

I touched her shoulder. Priscilla turned around and hit me so quick in the face that I fell back stunned. She got off Dong, leapt toward me like a little panther. She bared her golden teeth and for a second I was afraid she might bite me. But she just started hitting my head with her palms. I raised my arms for protection, her blows short and stinging, but I also found myself laughing the whole time, taken aback by the intensity of the little girl's rage.

"Apologize!" she screamed again and again and again.

"Okay, okay," I managed to say after a while. "Sorry. You win. Mercy already."

"God, girlie," Dong said, getting up, wiping the dirt from his pants with both hands. "Give peace a chance."

She stopped. She looked at us both. "I told you I'd kill you," she said proudly, crossing her arms. And then she reached out and punched Dong in the shoulder. "Fuck," Dong said, flinching. "All right already. You know, it's a good thing you're a girl because—"

"You didn't say sorry," she interrupted him sternly. Dong rubbed his shoulder with a hand. She raised her fists again.

"Okay," he grunted. "Sorry. Happy now?"

"No," she said. "Now I want you to say sorry to my mama."

"No way," I said.

"Fuck no," said Dong, shaking his head, but Priscilla had already yelled something in Cambodian toward the shack and her mother was already walking slowly across the knoll, wiping her hands on a greasy apron.

Priscilla's mother was the shortest woman I'd ever seen, barely a head taller than us, with a face as flat as an omelet, wide black unreflective eyes, and a man's broad shoulders. Her teeth weren't gold like her daughter's. They were just slightly crooked, a bit yellow, boring and regular. Priscilla said something else to her in Cambodian. Her mother nodded, scowling at us silently the whole time. "Say you're sorry," Priscilla said in Thai.

Dong looked at me. I looked at Dong.

"Do it," she said, her face creasing into a severe frown. "Or I'll beat you again."

"Sorry," we finally said in unison, staring at each other's feet. Priscilla's mother kept on scowling at us. I thought she'd start barking in Cambodian. I thought we might even discover what ungodly thing she'd meant to do with that rusted shovel. She'd probably bury us alive, I thought. I got ready to run. But instead Priscilla's mother just reached out and slapped us lightly on the back of our heads. And then, to our surprise, she smiled at us broadly—a genuine smile—before saying something to Priscilla. And then she walked back down to the shack.

Priscilla eyed us curiously, picked at her golden teeth with a pinky nail, as if deciding what to do with us.

"Can we go now?" Dong asked.

"If you want," Priscilla said, shrugging. "Unless you guys want something to eat."

That was the beginning of a nice thing. We never threw rocks at her house again. Although Dong continued to insist that we hadn't fought back because Priscilla was just a little girl, I think we both knew there was little we could've done that afternoon to beat back her angry advances. She was so pissed off it was the purest expression of fury I'd ever witnessed aside from the night Mother took a broomstick to a gigantic rat that had been raiding our trash.

So we didn't mind when Priscilla showed up at the pool the next morning. We gladly took her in. The three of us would horse around aimlessly down there, wasting those bright summer days. That's when Priscilla told us about her father and her teeth. That's when Dong and I would look into her mouth and tell her she was rich.

We initiated Priscilla to the simple pleasures of a normal, non-refugee-camp summer. We introduced her to ice cream. We bought a kite and flew it from the bottom of the pool. We took her to a movie at the cheap theater in Onnut— a horror movie about some witch living by a canal—and Priscilla gripped me so hard during the frightening parts that I discovered tiny bruises on my forearms when we got out. We even taught her how to ride a bike. The first time she got going on her own, zoomed down the slope to the deep end, she screamed so loud you could almost feel the pool's porcelain walls vibrate.

For our part, Dong and I got better with the bike. We managed to pop a couple of wheelies, though the diving board trick was still far out of reach. "You guys are so stupid," Priscilla would say, watching us work up the courage to try again.

"That's the dumbest thing I've ever seen." But then she'd laugh so hard after we fell that it was almost worth risking our necks just to hear her guffaw.

When it got too hot we'd go to Priscilla's shack. Her mother cleaned houses in the nicer development down the road from ours—where the Thicknecks frolicked in their Olympic-sized community pool—but on days off Priscilla's mother would often make sticky rice for us. There was never more than that, no fish or pork or anything, but the rice felt good and substantial to have in the stomach. Priscilla's mother watched us eat impassively and the three of us would teach her a few Thai phrases. Dong and I taught her how to swear in Thai. We'd laugh because there was nothing funnier than hearing a flat-faced Cambodian refugee woman saying "Dickwad" and "Fuckface" and "Hairy beaver."

That's when we learned about Priscilla's name. She was named after Elvis Presley's wife. One of the few possessions her mother brought with her was an LP showing Elvis's fat farang mug framed by those thick bushy chops. The record sat on top of a milk crate, propped against the dirty tin wall like a centerpiece to a shrine, and although Priscilla said she'd never heard the record—they didn't own a player—her mother had done renditions during nights at the camps to get her to sleep. Dong and I looked at the LP cover and said we didn't understand how anybody could think the guy was handsome. If he grew up in Bangkok he wouldn't be king of anything. The

Thicknecks would probably call him names. He'd be no bet-ter than the rest of us plebes. "Look at the guy," we said. "He's wearing a cape."

Aside from the Elvis record, there was also a small pic-ture of Priscilla's father taped above the moth-eaten pallet she shared with her mother every night. In the picture, Priscilla's father stood before a massive concrete building wearing light green hospital scrubs. He had large, clunky glasses, stared intently at something outside the frame. "Now that guy there," we told Priscilla. "That guy's handsome. Elvis is puke compared to that guy." Priscilla believed her father was still alive. We weren't about to suggest otherwise.

The Cambodian shanty grew just as Father predicted. They really did move in packs. There were four, then six, then eight shacks and near the end of the summer there must have been thirty Cambodians living across the railroad tracks bordering our housing development. Their tiny houses leaned haphazardly against one another; from afar their shanty looked like a single delicate structure made of crinkled tin cards. Like Priscilla and her mother, they were mostly women and children, though a few dark, gaunt men appeared as well. The Cambodians never seemed to say much to each other, and when they did they spoke in hushed tones, as if being refugees also meant being quiet. They might turn blue with laughter or gesticulate wildly or get angry at each other, but they always seemed to do so at half the normal human vol-ume. During the evenings they chatted, kicked around a takraw ball, sewed blankets and pillows, tended to the herb garden they'd started planting in the knoll. Dong and I never spoke to any of them, but we thought it was nice the way they nodded or waved or smiled when we came by on our bikes.

Every morning a white pickup truck would arrive to take some of the Cambodians to work at a road construction site. They'd pile in back, bunched together so close there wasn't any room to sit. Once, Dong and I got up early enough to see this, and there was something about the faces of those Cambodians going to work that nearly broke our hearts in half. Their quiet anxious expressions said they weren't sure they were coming back. They looked at their dilapidated little world by the railroad tracks as if for the very last time. The truck would drop them off in the early evening and they would all be there, of course—nothing to worry about at all—and it was almost understandable to me how they could look relieved to be back at such shitty little shacks. Surviving each day seemed a victory and a wonder to them.

Two of Priscilla's teeth came out that summer. The first was a lateral incisor, close to her front teeth. She cried all day when she discovered it loosening from her gums. "I don't know what to do," she said, a finger holding the tooth in place. By that time Dong and I were already veterans of the ordeal. We told her not to worry. We told her it was natural. "I don't care if it's natural," she said, and then she cried and cried some more. We spent most of the morning consoling her. We told her to imagine the things she and her mother would be able to buy with the gold. A television. A record player. A refrigerator. But she said she didn't want anything. "It's my tooth," she said. "It's mine." Then I told her it had probably been her father's plan all along—he probably thought Priscilla and her mother would need the gold to find their way home to him— and the idea seemed to console her momentarily.

A week later, the tooth came out at last. We were sharing a bag of fishballs at the pool when Priscilla suddenly spat the tooth into her hand. We stared for a while at that ingot sitting in a small pool of spittle and blood and masticated fish, then Priscilla wiped it off and passed it around. The tooth didn't seem so brilliant outside of her mouth. It just looked like a shiny little pebble, impossibly light in my hand. We took the tooth back to Priscilla's mother and she put it away in a teakwood box next to Elvis Presley's portrait.

The housing development's decline became painfully visible, just as my parents had predicted. For the first time the development company didn't bother to fill the gaping potholes created by the wet-season floods. There were so many craters in the roads Mother said she was beginning to think we lived on the moon. She said, "Dear God, I really don't care about the health club or the pool or the community garden anymore, I just want to ride my bike to the bus stop without breaking my goddamn neck."

More rats started appearing as well. There were so many of them by the end of the summer that Mother could not have prevented them from getting to our trash even at her angriest. I watched in horror one evening as a mangy, mean-looking stray nosed a sewer grate outside our house only to scurry away frightened when three rats came lumbering out to greet her. "It's an invasion out there," Mother said. "It's a goddamn rat apocalypse." Father set poisoned rat-paper in the outdoor kitchen every other night. In the morning, there'd always be two or three rats, large as small kittens, squealing and moaning, struggling against the glutinous surface like demonic little dinosaurs dying in some tar pit.

Dong said rats were super-horny. He'd seen some documentary about it on television. One rat, he said, can make up to fifteen thousand little rats in a single year. Priscilla laughed and said this was nothing. "This is easy," she said. She told us that at one of the camps things got so bad people went to sleep hugging a stick just in case.

We discovered a rat in the pool one day. It had fallen in and couldn't find a way out. We stood at the edge of the pool staring at the hideous red-eyed thing prancing around. We didn't know what to do. So we wandered aimlessly for the rest of the morning. Dong seemed so upset about the rat I thought he'd start crying. But when we went back later that afternoon it was gone. We never saw a rat in there again. But the pool was different for us after that.

Father blamed the rats on the refugees. He said they always brought vermin with them. "It's no wonder about the rats," he said one night when some of the men in the development came over for drinks. "Those people shit and piss wherever they please. You can't have people shitting and pissing wherever they please and not expect to have rats."

The men nodded along, passed around a flask of rye. Dong's father was there as well. I brought over a tray full of Heinekens and a pail of fresh ice for the men while Mother sat in the kitchen getting angry at the checkbook.

"They're probably raising them," one of the men said. "Cambodians probably think rats are a delicacy."

"Cambodians," somebody else scoffed. "They're the real rats, if you ask me."

I poured the men their beer, emptied the ashtray into a plastic bag. Father put his hand on my shoulder. "This is my boy," Father said, shaking my shoulder vigorously. "This here's our future. This is who we're fighting for."

The men nodded drunkenly along. A chill passed through my body right then. I wanted to tell the men that the refugees had built a proper outhouse hidden discreetly behind a hedge. I wanted to tell them that they didn't shit and piss indiscriminately like Father had said. I wanted to tell them about Priscilla and her mother. But I didn't think the men would appreciate these revelations.

I woke up late that night to the sound of their high, excited voices. I got out of bed and watched them standing around my father in the yard, nodding their heads in unison. Somebody arrived with a pickup truck and the men climbed in, their deep, drunken voices murmuring up to my window. They left their empty bottles on the straw mat in our yard, and for some reason I thought about how Mother and I would have to pick up the mess in the morning. The truck puttered down the street, the men chanting now, as if working up the courage to do something valiant. I walked down the stairs with my heart in my mouth. I threw on my rubber slippers, started running into the night, down the street and out toward the railroad tracks.

Halfway there, winded from running, I saw all I needed to see. The men were torching the Cambodian shantytown. A light red glow bloomed at the end of the development's main street, like a second sun rising in the night. I heard gruff, exasperated voices, the high-pitched screams of women. Something exploded. Glass shattered. Somebody yelled profanities. I stopped walking then and sat cross-legged in the middle of the street. I watched a rat scuttle into a sewer grate, appear once more to forage for food. Watching that awful red flickering in the distance, I felt so weak and dizzy that if the rats had emerged to eat me alive I couldn't have done a thing to stop them.

I don't remember walking home. But I must have, because I woke up in my own bed the next morning, head throbbing with pain. I thought I was losing my mind. I tried to convince myself that I had dreamt the previous night's events, but when I embraced Father that morning he reeked of smoke and gasoline.

I went to Dong's house immediately after breakfast. I tried to tell him about it, but Dong stopped me halfway and said he already knew. He told me his father had also smelled like gasoline. He said all the fathers in our development smelled like gasoline this morning.

"It happens," Dong said. "What can you do? They had it coming. It was only a matter of time. My pa said it wasn't even their land. He said you can't live for free like that, it's really not fair to the rest of us."

"What about Priscilla?"

"What about Priscilla?" Dong repeated. "She'll be fine. She's a survivor."

"I can't believe this," I said. "I can't believe I'm best friends with a fat, knock-kneed asshole."

"Hey," Dong said. "Watch it, fucker."

Then he turned around and went back inside the house. I stood there gaping at his front door, shaking with fury. I didn't know what to do. I wanted to hurt him. So I went over and took his bike from the yard. Dong screamed at me from his window but I was already pumping away at the pedals, racing toward what was left of the shantytown to find Priscilla and her mother.

Bits of ash swirled around the railroad tracks. A thin veil of smoke hung in the air, stinging my eyes. When I arrived, it was as if the Cambodians' shanty had never existed. There wasn't a shack left standing. The ground smoldered with blackened sheets of tin. Their herb garden, too, had been razed. All the Cambodians stood around picking through the rubble, muttering to one another quietly in the early morning sun. Fortunately, some of their possessions had been saved; they piled bags and belongings together on a small patch of clean ground. Nobody looked particularly panicked. Nobody seemed particularly sad. It was as if they'd expected the fire. But nobody acknowledged me when I arrived.

Priscilla stood with her mother next to the Cambodians' stuff. The other women milled around them waving smoke from their faces. Her mother sat on a knapsack and stared at the rubble, a bored look on her face. She seemed to look right through me at first, but then she nodded seriously. Priscilla smiled when I arrived. She had dark rings around her eyes and her face was blackened from the fire, like somebody had smeared it with charcoal. "Hey," she said. "Hey," I said, panting, throwing Dong's bike to the ground. "This really sucks, girlie."

She told me that nobody had been particularly hurt. She and her mother hadn't lost too much. The golden tooth, the Presley album, the picture of Priscilla's father—all had survived the fire, though they'd have to find a new pallet to sleep on. Priscilla said the men had come banging on their houses with sticks last night, told them to get out before they burned them alive in their shacks. I listened, nodded along, tried to look like she was telling me something I didn't already know.

I told her I was glad she and her mother weren't hurt, but I could barely look at her. Priscilla shook her head and said the same thing had happened at the last place they'd squatted. Just like Dong, she told me it was only a matter of time. She said it could've been a lot worse.

"We're leaving," she said finally. "We're going. I'm gonna miss you guys."

She looked at Dong's bike and asked me where he was. I told her he was sleeping. I invited Priscilla to the half-finished pool one last time. She asked her mother if she could go and her mother nodded silently, told Priscilla to be back in an hour. Before we left, I went up to Priscilla's mother and apologized. It seemed I was always apologizing to that short, flat-faced woman. It seemed, too, that I'd never be able to apologize enough. "I'm very sorry about your house," I said in Thai, and once more Priscilla's mother slapped me on the back of the head, smiled widely out of that omelet face. "Hairy Beaver," she answered in Thai. "Dickwad. Fuckface."

We didn't do much at the pool that morning. We just sat around with our feet dangling off the edge chatting about this and that, the weather getting hotter and hotter. If we lived in a better world, I would've ridden that bike off the diving board and landed perfectly in the deep end for Priscilla. She could've remembered me by that. But it didn't feel like a morning for bike tricks; it didn't feel like a morning for clowning around. Priscilla was tired, uncharacteristically quiet. She hadn't slept all night. Another incisor was coming out. She showed me, nudged it lightly with a finger, the golden tooth wobbling to and fro on her short pink gums. I stared at it transfixed because I knew that this would be the last time I'd peer into Priscilla's golden mouth.

We made our way back to the smoldering shanty. To my surprise, Dong was there when we arrived, chatting with Priscilla's mother. We didn't acknowledge one another. The Cambodians were gathering their belongings, getting ready to leave. I went with Priscilla to her mother, listened to them talk for a while, tried to ignore Dong standing beside me. It suddenly made me nauseated being around the Cambodians.

Priscilla was asking for something in a pleading voice. Her mother nodded, looked at her sternly, looked over at Dong and me every so often. They were arguing about something. But then, after her mother nodded once more, Priscilla skipped excitedly to their knapsack and dug out the teakwood box.

"This is for you," she said, putting the tooth in one of Dong's hands. Dong looked at me for the first time. "I can't take this, girlie," he said, shaking his head, extending his open palm back to her.

"It's for you and your mama," Priscilla said, closing his fingers around the tooth. "Take it or I'll beat you again." Dong shrugged. "Okay," he said, shoving the tooth into a pocket. "Thanks a lot, girlie."

She looked at me. I was next. I wanted to tell her no. I wanted to stop her. But Priscilla was already working away at that incisor, wobbling it back and forth with a thumb and a forefinger, her face contorted in pain and concentration. All the Cambodians stopped, looked over at Priscilla and me. She seemed to work at that incisor for an unbearably long time. I could hardly look at her do it. And then with a strong, vigorous gesture she got the tooth free at last, and there was a small gap now where there should've been gold, a smidgen of light red blood on her gums.

"And this is for you," she said, wiping the tooth clean on her pants, handing me the thing. I took it, put it in my back pocket. I thanked her. And then she went over and helped maneuver the large knapsack onto her mother's back.

We never heard from Priscilla the Cambodian again. Those, too, were the last days Dong and I spent together. Soon after, Dong's parents sold their duplex back to the development company for half the original price. My parents eventually did the same for even less money.

That day, however, Dong and I stood by their ruined shantytown and watched them walk away, their figures getting smaller and smaller by the minute. But then, wordlessly, I decided I couldn't watch them leave. I walked over to Dong's bike and picked it off the ground.

"Hey," he said. "Give me my bike, you asshole."

"You fat fuck," I said, scrambling onto the seat. "Come get it yourself."

I started pumping away at the pedals again, standing upright, the wind blowing quickly through my hair, Dong's exasperated voice trailing off behind me. I don't know how long

I biked that morning. In my mind, I'd decided to bike to the ends of the earth. The development flew by. I biked past its limits, out onto Pattanakan Road, past the Thicknecks' pristine development. I crossed through the fresh market. The streets and the people became stranger by the minute. I biked through thick traffic, smoke and exhaust whipping around me, cars honking every so often as I maneuvered haphazardly between them. I climbed over the bridge spanning some wide black canal. I went farther from my house that morning than I'd ever been on my own. I kept biking until the sun rose high in the sky and my body quivered from exhaustion and my thighs burned as they'd never burned before.

I stopped at an intersection; men and women in business suits looked at me sternly as they walked by. I didn't know where the hell I was. I didn't know how long I'd been biking. I needed to get to a bathroom. I needed to piss; I needed to vomit as well. I left Dong's bike by a telephone booth and went into a noodle shop. The owner eyed me curiously over steaming vats of broth. He asked me what I wanted. I could tell that he thought I was some street urchin. I didn't say anything. I just marched to the back of the shop and slipped into the bathroom before the owner could stop me. In the bathroom, as I was urinating, I remembered the tooth Priscilla gave me. I threw that keepsake into the toilet bowl. I flushed. I decided I couldn't keep a thing like that.

When I emerged from the bathroom, the owner was waiting for me, frowning severely. "What the hell are you doing, kid?" he asked me.

"I was taking a piss," I said. "What did you think I was doing?"

He reached out and tried to grab me by the collar. I slipped from his grasp just in time. I tried to punch him in the stomach. But he'd reached out to grab my wrists—one, then the other. His hands were strong. He gripped me hard and pulled me toward him. All the strength left my body, and my eyes suddenly felt hot with tears. I was crying, though I hadn't realized it until then.

The owner of the noodle shop knelt down to look me in the eyes.

"I'm not one to thrash another man's child," he whispered through gritted teeth. I felt my hands getting numb from his grip. I tried to writhe away but the more I struggled, the harder his hands held me in place, his thick fingernails digging into my skin.

"So this is what we're gonna do," he said. "We're gonna pretend that you didn't just try to punch me. I'm gonna let you go and I'm gonna count to three. By the time I get to three, you're gonna be gone. You're gonna go back to wherever the hell you just came from. You understand me, boy?"

I started crying in earnest then, the tears streaming freely down my face, mucus salty on my lips.

"Let me go," I whimpered. "Please."

"I'm not running a goddamn orphanage here, kid," he continued, still gripping me. "I'm not running a public rest room, either. I'm running a business, you understand me?"

He stared at me for a while, his face contorted with exasperation.

"You understand me?" he asked again.

"Yes, sir," I stammered. "I understand you, sir."

"Good," he said, letting go of my wrists. "One. Two. Three."

DON'T LET ME DIE
IN THIS PLACE

My son Jack says I'm being difficult. It's dinnertime. It's hot as hell. The mongrel children are kicking each other under the table, yapping and giggling senselessly. The wife's coming at me with spoonfuls of cold, clumpy porridge. Each time the spoon hovers close to my face my foreign daughter-in-law opens her mouth like she's instructing me by example. I hate it when she does this. It's demeaning. I know how to eat, thank you very much. And while I've learned to accept with dignity the fact that I can't really feed myself anymore—and while, hell, I've even learned to live with wearing a bib during meals—every time my son's wife opens her mouth like that it's almost enough to set my dead right arm to shaking.

"Jack, please tell her to stop," I say, the spoon so close I could lick it, the wife with her lips parted stupidly again. "Tell her I hate it when she opens her mouth like that." But my son just gapes at me, sighs, and says, "Don't be difficult, Father," like I'm some child misbehaving in a department store.

The wife looks at me, looks at Jack, shoves the spoon back into the porridge bowl. She gets up from the table. The mongrels quiet down for the first time all evening. "Enough," the wife says in English to my son, throwing up her hands. "I no do this no more, okay? He eat by himself now, Jack." Jack sighs again, calls after the wife by her name. He says, "Tida—," but she's already halfway out of the kitchen, muttering to herself in Thai like some crazy.

Jack blinks at me, frowning. "Nice," he says, getting up to follow her. "Mission accomplished, Father."

"What? What the hell did I do now?"

But my son just throws down his napkin and goes to fetch his Thai wife. Soon it's just the mongrels and me staring at each other. A mosquito buzzes in my ear. I reach out with my good left hand to swat it. I miss. The only thing I manage to kill in that ear is the hearing. I watch the girl say something to the little boy in Thai. The boy looks at me wide-eyed. "Stop," I tell them, though neither of my grandchildren speak much English. "You shouldn't stare. It's rude."

To my surprise they seem to understand because they start looking at their half-empty plates like they've suddenly cultivated an interest in china. So I sit for a while and look at my foreign grandchildren trying not to look at me. I try to get my hearing back, pick at the assaulted eardrum with my good left hand. I glance over at the bowl of porridge, and suddenly I'm hungrier than I've been in a very long time.

* * *

Jack's washing my back with a coarse sponge. Given the evening's events, my son's scrubbing me quite hard tonight. I'm rocking from the brash, rough motion. I feel a little bad about things—the wife never came back to dinner—so I try to keep quiet. But there's only so much passive-aggressive scrubbing a man can take from his only son.

"Dammit, Jack," I finally say. "Clean me. Don't skin me."

He stops. He comes around and starts wiping down my torso. He doesn't look me in the eye. Jack hates to look when I bathe. He's embarrassed by my nakedness. If there's anybody who should be embarrassed it's probably me. He's not the one who can't bathe himself.

"What's it going to take, Father?" he says now, directly at my navel, the sponge cold and prickly against the folds of my stomach. "What's it going to take for you to be happy here?" He squeezes the sponge over my shoulders. Water dribbles down my chest. I wipe at it with my good left hand. "Good question, Jack," I say. "You always ask good questions."

He laughs. It's not a good laugh. It's a grunting, impatient sound.

"Dying would be good," I say finally. "Dying would make me pretty happy."

"Father—"

"I bet it would probably make you all a lot happier too."

"Christ."

"Well, maybe not you, Jack, but certainly that wife of yours," I say. "She'd probably throw a party. That woman hates me. I know she does. Why, Jack? Why does she hate me? I'm just an old man, you know. I'm very fragile."

"She doesn't hate you, Father."

"Of course she does," I say. "Just look at tonight. All I did was put in an honest request and she makes a scene. I swear, Jack, that woman's trying to give me another goddamn stroke. She'll kill me with her hate one of these days."

"You're incredible," Jack says, shaking his head. He mutters something else under his breath, soaps my thighs, wipes at my legs with the sponge. He's working fast now, like he can't wait to get the whole thing over with, scrubbing in that rough, unpleasant way again. I stare at the top of his head for a while. It's all depressing me to no end. I feel like furniture. So I look at the shower walls, search for pictures in the mildew like they're clouds in the sky. I make out a herd of wild horses galloping across the linoleum. This turns out to be a bad idea because it makes me think of Macklin Johnson back home— that poor, beautiful man—and how we used to sit around and rent old Spaghetti Westerns to pass the time, and suddenly something hot and awful blooms in my chest and my eyes start to well up involuntarily.

"Jesus," Jack says. "Don't tell me you're gonna cry now."

What can a grown man say to such a thing? My son wipes down my face. He's helping me into my clothes. He's carrying me to the electric wheelchair, his arms like tight ropes around my shoulders and legs. I'm still thinking of Mac. I'm still steeling myself against tears. "Jack," I say, swallowing hard. My son straps me in, positions the lame arm across my lap. "C'mon now," he says, smiling at me for the first time all evening. "Buck up, old man. Things will get better. Nobody hates you here."

"Jack," I say again. "I want to go home. Don't let me die in this place."

"You're not going to die, Father," my son says. "You're going to be happy."

I'm trying to get some sleep, still thinking of old Mac, when the wife peers into my room and scares me so bad I nearly crap my pajamas. She stands in the doorway, her small silhouette dark and ominous, and says in a meek voice, "Mister Perry sleeping?" and I say, "No, woman. Mister Perry's pole-vaulting. Mister Perry's running a goddamn marathon. What else do you think Mister Perry's doing?"

She stands there silently, cocks her head curiously to one side.

"What do you want from me?" I ask after a while.

"I no want nothing." Her voice is a little louder now. "I just want to say sorry to you. I no mean to make you upset."

"Who said I was upset?"

"Jack tell me you cry."

"That's a lie," I say.

"No lie." She's shaking her head. "Jack say you crying like baby in the shower."

"That's ridiculous. I think I would know if I was crying or not, woman."

She's silent for a moment. She shoves her hands into her pockets like she doesn't know what to do with them. "Well," she says. "I'm sorry for tonight."

"Apology accepted then."

"But in the future," she adds sternly, "if you desire to say something to me you just say it to me, okay? Don't say to Jack. I speak English. Not so good, but I understand what you say."

"Sure," I say. "You speak English."

She stands there a while longer like she's waiting for me to apologize as well. But I don't have anything to apologize about. I wasn't the one infantilizing a helpless old man during dinner. So I say, "Turn up the fan, Tida. I'm melting in here." For a second, I think she might make another scene, but instead she walks over to the fan and kicks it up a notch. It turns on its axle like some creature shaking its head slowly from side to side.

"Thanks," I say, the fan's cool breeze tickling my face. "That's better."

She walks across the room, stands over the bed, looks down at me for a while. I think she might strangle me, but instead she just pulls the sheets up under my chin.

"Okay?"

"Okay," I say.

"Tomorrow will be better, Mister Perry."

"I doubt it," I say, closing my eyes. "But let's hope so."

When I open my eyes again the wife's gone. The hallway light is off. It's quiet in the house and I'm staring in the dark thinking about the last time I saw Macklin Johnson.

We had tickets for an Orioles game. The tickets were his going-away present for me. He was coming over to pick me up. Things already weren't going so good for the two of us by then. I'd had my little episode and Mac was starting to get confused. His memory was starting to deteriorate. We'd been seeing each other less and less, what with Mac's forgetfulness and me sitting at home lamenting my condition, trying to figure out the fancy wheelchair, doing my damnedest not to get into high-speed collisions with the furniture.

So I was happy that Mac got the Orioles tickets. It was a nice gesture. It seemed a way to say good-bye. But I was not so happy about having to remind him every other day about why he'd gotten them.

"So we're going to a baseball game," he'd said the week before our date.

"Yeah," I replied. "You bought the damn tickets, Mac."

"Oh. So why are we going?"

"Because I'm leaving, remember? I'm going to go live with Jack and his wife."

"You're leaving? Where the hell you going, Perry? You can't even get to your front porch these days."

"Thailand. Bangkok."

"That's a damn shame. I'll miss you."

"Yeah."

"What the hell's Jack doing over there anyway? He get drafted?"

"Beats me. He's working in textiles, I think."

"Perry, you know I fucking hate baseball. It's a stupid game. Never understood what the big deal was."

So, naturally, I had my doubts about whether Mac would show up on the appointed day. But he did. He was right on time. He rolled up in his old Volkswagen, got out of the van, and it was a beautiful thing to watch him walk up my front steps in one of his old pinstriped suits. He and Patricia—the black nurse who came by every morning—helped me into the van. "Be careful," Patricia said before we left. "Don't get into trouble. You drive real slow, you hear, Mister Johnson?"

As we got on the highway toward Baltimore it seemed like everything might actually be all right. Mac seemed lucid. He was making sense. He nattered on about his own live-in and how much he liked her, how much better she was than the last one, how she was real beautiful and tall, like an African princess, and how irritated she'd gotten that morning when he said she looked like Nefertiti.

"I don't get it," he said. "A man can't even compliment a beautiful woman these days." Mac'd always had a thing for black women. He'd married two, the last one, Carmen—a real elegant lady with a wonderful smile—having died two years before from cancer in the head. "I didn't say she looked like Aunt Jemima, you know," Mac continued. "I'd understand if she got mad about *that*. All I said was Nefertiti and, wow, slap me silly and call me an asshole."

I nodded along, pulled the old ballcap snug over my head with my good left hand. But then I realized we'd passed up the exit to Camden Yards.

"Hey," I said. "There's Camden Yards, Mac."

He looked over at me and smiled. That's when I got real scared.

"We're not going to Camden Yards, Perry," he said, laughing. "You know I fucking hate baseball. Never understood what the big deal was."

"Jesus, Macklin," I said. "C'mon now. Don't joke around."

"What?" he said. "Aren't we going to Hopkins? Aren't we going to visit Carmen?"

"No, Mac. Carmen's dead. We're going to an Orioles game."

"Oh," he said, and now he looked not only confused, he also looked ashamed. "That's why you're wearing the ballcap."

But Mac didn't turn the car around. We kept on zipping along that highway. "I knew that, you know," he said. "I knew that about Carmen. You didn't have to remind me, Perry."

"Take me home, Macklin."

"Really?"

"Yes," I said. "I just want to go home now."

"You sure?"

"Yeah. Let's just go rent some videos."

It took us a while to get back to the house, me directing Mac the whole time thinking I was living my last hour on this earth. Patricia was still at the house cleaning. She came out and helped me get out of the van and into the wheelchair. She didn't seem the least bit surprised to see us back so soon. She didn't even ask about the game. I told Mac to come inside. While he sat in the living room, I called his son Tyrone out in Bethesda.

"Jesus," Tyrone said. "You know he shouldn't be driving, Mister Perry."

"No, I didn't, son," I said. "I really thought he was all right."

Tyrone arrived by train a few hours later. When I said good-bye to Mac, he suddenly became lucid again. He bent down and hugged me real hard.

"Hey," he said. "I'm real sorry about today, Perry. But you come back soon, okay? I'll make it up to you. The world ain't seen the last of us yet."

He climbed into the Volkswagen with his son and that was the last I ever saw of my friend. That's the last I'll probably ever see of him. Because I'm lying here now six weeks later in this bed, in this hot, godforsaken, mosquito-infested country, thousands of miles away from ever seeing another Orioles game, with two grandchildren I can barely talk to, a daughter-in-law who mocks my paralysis during mealtimes, and a son who seems indifferent to my plight, all of them sleeping soundly in this house, dreaming their nice little dreams, and I'm so pissed off I'm making a fist in the dark with my good left hand.

Alice would know what to do with the mongrel grandchildren. But Alice isn't here. Alice is long gone. She never even met these kids sitting across from me now playing a game of gin rummy to help their grandfather pass the time. She never had to deal with the little girl being cute, cheating, spying at my hand through the reflection on my bifocals. Alice never got to slap the girl lightly on the head and say, "Hey. Stop that. Don't set a bad example for your little brother. We aren't a cheating people." She never got to see the girl stare at her uncomprehendingly and then lay down her final trick—four jacks—slamming the rummy card facedown, raising her little cheating fists in victory, sticking out a tongue to taunt her half-paralyzed grandfather while her younger brother laughs with unabashed glee.

"I kick Grandfather ass," the girl says in English, grinning her cheater's grin.

"Don't say that," I tell her, throwing down my hand in disgust. "Nice girls don't say 'ass.'"

"Ass ass ass," the little boy hisses, giggling hysterically at the sound of his own voice.

"But you teach me," the girl says. "You teach me 'ass,' yes?"

"No, I didn't. I'd never teach you that."

"Yes, you did," she says. "You teach. You say to me one day, 'Your father Jack is one ass.'"

"Well," I say. "Even if I did, you shouldn't say it. Only old men like me get to use that word."

"Ass ass ass!" the boy continues yapping. He gets up and does a little dance by the table to accompany his refrain. "Shut up," I tell him. "Sit down, boy." But he doesn't listen. He just chants his way to the kitchen to find his mother. "No more play today," the girl says, getting up from the table to follow her brother. "But maybe tomorrow. Maybe tomorrow Grandfather will win. Maybe tomorrow Grandfather ass will be okay."

"And maybe tomorrow," I mutter, watching her skip happily through the doorway to the kitchen, "you'll stop being such a goddamn cheat."

When Alice died Jack had been a year in Bangkok. He'd become an executive at some Japanese factory. He was still a bachelor. We rarely heard from him. I think my wife died half-convinced our son was a homosexual. When Jack came back for the funeral and told me he was getting married to a Thai woman, I became belligerent. I told him the news might've saved his mother's life. I didn't really mean it, of course. I was just sad and angry and scared about Alice dying. I was already starting to miss her pretty bad. But I don't think Jack has ever forgiven me for saying that. Macklin Johnson told me they never forgive you for saying things like that.

I've fallen asleep facedown at the table. They're waking me up. The wife peels a two of clubs from my cheek and the children laugh. She sits me upright in my chair, clears the cards, sets the table for lunch. "Mister Perry," she says. "We eat."

It's rice and fried egg today. I don't really want the wife to feed me, but the last time I insisted on feeding myself I'd poured chicken broth down my shirt collar. In due time, with enough exercise and practice, the doctors say, I'll regain my dignity. They say I'll be able to use my good left hand just as I'd been able to use my right. But I've been lifting that five-pound barbell for weeks now and the hand still shakes like it's got a life of its own.

Fortunately, the wife feeds me in a respectful, close-mouthed way today, dabbing at the corners of my lips with a cloth napkin. Ever since I got here I've been having drool-management problems. I've been a leaky faucet.

"You feel better today, Mister Perry?" she asks, and I say, in between bites, sucking back the spittle pooling at my gums, "Yeah. I feel like a million bucks, woman."

I'm not that hungry. Halfway through the meal I shake my head and the wife starts eating her own meal. As always, it's hot as hell. My stomach's sweating clean through my shirt. For a while I just sit there and stare at the kids spooning clumsily at their fried rice and egg, talking to each other in Thai, the wife nodding now and again at something they say.

Neither of the children look much like me. I have to look real hard to find any resemblances. They have broad flat noses, long banana-shaped eyes, dark auburn hair, and clear toffee-colored skin. None of them look much like Jack, either, though the boy's eyes are Jack's brown-speckled blue and they've both inherited my son's thin lips and strong square jaw. But these are attributes Jack himself inherited from Alice. There's actually not much of me in Jack so I suppose it makes sense there isn't much of me in these kids. Still. I have to remind myself sometimes that they're not adopted, that these children are my own flesh and blood, that somewhere in their little brown bodies some brilliant characteristic of mine might reveal itself in due time, even if I have trouble pronouncing their names and they have trouble pronouncing mine. (My name's oftentimes a verb on their tongues—*Parry*—sometimes even an adjective—*Purry*—like I'm a cat—so I've made them call me "Grandfather" instead. I rarely say their names at all. I call the girl "girl" and the boy "boy," since the few times I tried calling them by their real names, "Ruchira" and "Sornram," they'd both laughed insensitively at my attempts.)

Now I'm not saying people shouldn't mix. The heart will do what the heart needs to do. And Macklin Johnson is my best friend in the whole world. But at least Mac can see himself in Tyrone and the grandchildren. At least he can call them by name. At least they all speak a common language. At least Mac can look at them and say, "Yes, you're my son, you're my grandchildren, you all came from my own flesh and my own blood," though given his condition lately he's probably starting to confuse them all. At least Macklin Johnson isn't stuck in this tropical jungle of a city wondering how the hell these people—his only living heirs—could be even remotely related to him.

But I don't really mind the mongrels. I'm actually dreading the day they have to go back to school. Even if they don't say much to me, it's nice to have them around. They keep me company while Jack's at work. I spend most days sitting in the wheelchair watching them play, lifting that five-pound barbell, dozing in and out of sleep.

My six-year-old grandson adores his older sister to the point of self-annihilation. He does whatever she tells him. He's the most gullible kid I've ever seen. Each day he happily submits himself to whatever new experiment in misery his sister comes up with. I'd like to teach him a little something about self-respect, but the way things are going right now I can barely communicate to him what time of day it is.

Today the girl's convinced him to be her pet dog for the afternoon. The boy's down on all fours. He's leading his sister around the house and the front yard with a long string of black yarn tied loosely around his neck, barking, sniffing the ground, panting happily at his sister. "Hey," I say to the girl, "that's not very nice," but she just blinks at me and says, "He *likes* it," the boy barking in agreement, so I leave them to it.

An hour later, the boy licks my left leg and the leg jerks back into his face as any man's leg would when he's half-asleep in his wheelchair.

The boy falls back, looks up at me for a moment, and then he starts to cry. The girl laughs, though she crouches down to see if her brother's okay. He's not. He's bleeding lightly from the nose.

"Oh shit," I say, bending forward in my seat. "You all right, boy?"

But he's already running upstairs to his mother, that string of yarn flying behind him like a kite's tail. The girl stands there shaking her head at me.

"Why?" she asks me in English. "Why Grandfather kick his ass?"

"I didn't kick his ass, girl. I kicked him in the face." For some reason I'm laughing. "Not funny, Grandfather," she says. "Ass. Face. Whatever. He *crying*."

"I know," I say. "I know. I didn't mean to. I was half-asleep. I didn't know what I was doing. It's your fault he was licking my leg in the first place, you know."

A few minutes later the wife's looming over me, the boy sniveling at her side. "What happen?" she asks me, frowning, and I try to tell her, but the boy keeps interrupting me, pointing and crying some more in Thai. He's got two humongous wads of toilet paper in his nostrils. She tries to quiet him down, crouches and gathers him in her arms. "You kick him?" she asks me, stroking the boy's head. "Why you kick his face, Mister Perry?"

"It was an accident," I say. "I was sleeping, Tida. I didn't mean to. They were playing a game and—" The girl interrupts me and says something to the mother in Thai, gesticulating with her arms. For a second I think she's framing me, because the wife looks at me severely. But then the wife smiles, hands the little boy over to his sister, and the children walk hand-in-hand out to the sunny front yard.

"He be okay, Mister Perry," the wife says. "He just scared."

"Tell him to come back, Tida," I say. "Tell him I want to say sorry. I didn't mean to kick him, you know."

"I know," she says. "But maybe later, Mister Perry. Right now he just frightened. You say sorry later, okay?"

But the boy avoids me for the rest of the day. He can't even look me in the eye. I try to make amends. I fold a paper airplane with my good left hand. But my hand's too shaky again and it turns out crumpled and lopsided. I do my best to toss it at the kids, but they both ignore the thing as it flops down between us. I even call the boy by his real name to get a laugh. The boy whispers something to his sister, they go get their badminton racquets, and then they both head out to play in the empty afternoon street. I'd like to watch them, but it's sweltering hot today and when I went outside last week I'd puked from the heat. So I just sit for the rest of the afternoon by the front door watching the feather shuttlecock sail up and down, back and forth, beyond the property wall, hoping Jack will come home soon to save me.

When I first arrived Jack and his family thought it would be a good idea to take me around the city. Jack took the week off work and we piled into the Corolla every morning. I'd sit up front in the passenger seat while Tida mediated peace between the children in back.

Given the city's traffic, we never went to more than a few places each day. I thought rush hour in Washington was awful, but Bangkok traffic makes downtown D.C. look like a Formula One racetrack. I don't remember much about that first week except spending most of my time staring listlessly out the passenger-side window, falling in and out of sleep, the car moving in tiny fits and starts the whole way. "It's a goddamn parking lot out here," I said the first day while we were stalled at a traffic light for what seemed like an hour.

Temples, temples, and more temples. That's all we ever went to the first few days. For some reason, Jack and his wife thought it would be useful for me to see them. The children weren't having too good a time and I didn't blame them— children and places of religious worship don't, as a rule, mix very well. They'd be bored to death, wringing their hands in the car, while Jack and the wife wheeled me inside to admire some temple. I wasn't having too good a time either. I would've preferred to sit in the cool, air-conditioned sedan with the kids. While I can certainly learn to appreciate cultural differences, if Tida and the children came to visit me in Washington and I took them on a tour of all the city's churches, I don't think they'd have a very good time either. So on the third morning, I told Jack that there's only so many temples a grown man can look at—no matter how beautiful or colorful or interesting the temples may be—and I told him that this city was just too goddamn hot for a man in my condition anyway. "Jack," I said, "I'm not some tourist, you know," and Jack said, "Fine, Father. Let's just stay home then. Let's just sit here and pretend like there isn't a world outside this house."

Truth be told, I also didn't enjoy the trips because they made me feel self-conscious. Back home in America, a man in my condition may leave his house and encounter the smug, pitying stares of his fellow human beings. It took me a while to learn to ignore that, but here in Thailand the same problem's compounded by the fact that these people like to *talk* about me. I complained to Jack once and he called me paranoid and narcissistic, but I just said, "Try getting paraded around in a wheelchair, Jack. Try that and see if you don't feel like they're talking about you."

So for the rest of the week we went to the local mall. Jack and I would go into the Cineplex and watch American action movies while the children accompanied Tida on her jaunts through the mall's various department stores. That wasn't so bad. It actually made me pretty happy. As the lights dimmed and the film started rolling, it felt like being back home for a few hours, especially once I learned to ignore the gaudy yellow subtitles. And it felt like old times between Jack and me. We were just father and son catching a flick together, and it was easy enough then to forget my troubles for a little while. It even seemed on occasion that when we emerged from the theater the world out there might be one we both knew well.

The children are still outside batting around the shuttlecock when Jack gets home. I tell him about kicking the boy. He laughs. He says, "Give it some time, Father. He's just a kid. He's probably already forgotten about it."

"You should've seen his face," I say. "He looked at me like I was a monster."

"Wait," Jack teases. "You're *not* a monster?"

"Very funny," I say. "I'm serious, Jack. I feel awful."

"Don't worry about it," Jack says. "You can kick him in the face a hundred times and he'd still be your grandson."

Tida's sitting at the dining room table doing the bills. Jack walks over and bends down to kiss her on the head. They speak to each other in Thai for a little while. It's strange and perplexing to hear Jack speak Thai. You grow old thinking you know your kid and then he suddenly starts speaking a foreign language and you never knew him at all.

I maneuver the wheelchair toward them, the electric engine wheezing beneath me.

"At least talk to him for me," I say, interrupting their conversation. "Tell him I'm sorry. Tell him I didn't mean to kick him in the face."

"All right," Jack says, smiling. "I'll have a little chat with him if it makes you feel better."

"No worry, Mister Perry," the wife intones. She puts a hand on my dead right arm. "Sornram okay. He just little boy."

I blink at the wife. She and Jack start talking again. Jack's telling her some story, maybe something funny about his day, because she laughs every so often at what he's saying. They seem happy with their own company, so I wheel myself over to my room.

It's a small gray room with concrete walls that they'd used as storage space before I got here. Jack said it's temporary. He said I'd have a room on the second floor once they retrofitted the stairs with some fancy contraption that's supposed to take me up there like a skier in a chairlift. I remember Mac installing one of those things so Carmen could get to the basement, but she'd died without ever getting to use it. Once, before my stroke—a little bored and a little drunk on sherry—Mac and I rode the thing and timed each other to see who could do it the fastest.

I think about writing Mac a letter but when I go to the computer they've set up for me I can't figure out how to turn it on. I also don't really know what to write; I can't see how he'd be interested in hearing about my grandson getting kicked in the face. Besides, I've already written Mac three letters and I've yet to receive a reply. So I close my eyes, thinking I might take a nap before dinner. I feel exhausted. I didn't get much sleep last night. But when I try to rest I keep seeing the boy's little face looking at me like I'd tried to destroy one of his beloved stuffed animals.

I hear the children come in the house at last. They're talking to their father. The girl laughs hysterically at something Jack's doing and the boy's voice sounds like he wants to participate too. The wife is laughing along with them, calling Jack's name in a teasing manner. I don't know what they're saying, I don't know what the hell they're doing out there, but they sound pretty much like a normal family from where I'm sitting and suddenly I'm smiling like some loony alone in his padded room.

I keep a picture of Alice by my bed. I pick it up. It's not a remarkable photo, just my Alice standing at the sink washing dishes, but there's something nice about the late evening light cascading through the vanilla drapes in front of her. Alice never liked having her picture taken. She couldn't see why we needed them. *Perry,* she'd said that day, laughing, when in my boredom I'd brought out the old Leica, *what am I going to do with a picture of myself?* And I remember telling her then that the picture wasn't for her, it was for me, so just shut up and give me your best smile, Alice, look beautiful for me, because when my mind goes I'm gonna need something to remember you by.

I put the picture back on the stand. It's a sauna in here. I feel like fainting. I feel like crying. When I look up, the little boy is standing in the doorway, peering in shyly at me.

"Hello," he says sheepishly. "How do you do?"

He's always asking me this. He learned a little English in the first grade, but that's the only phrase he seems to remember. He still has wads of toilet paper flaring from both his nostrils.

"How do you do?" he says again, like I hadn't heard him the first time.

"Hey," I say, turning the chair around. I wave him over. "Come here. Let me take a look at that nose."

He eyes me curiously, takes slow, cautious steps into my room. I reach out and hold his small chin up to the light with my good left hand. He looks confused, a little frightened by the gesture.

"You'll be all right," I say, inspecting his face. "Sorry about that."

When I let go the kid reaches out and hugs me so hard I almost fall out of the chair. He squeezes me tight around the neck and I can barely breathe. When he's done, he waves at me with both hands, says "Bye-bye," and then runs out of the room like he can't get away from me fast enough. I sit there listening to his footsteps pattering back to the dining room. A little later Jack pokes his head in the door and says, "Everything all right with the kid? Why are you sitting in the dark, Father?" and I say, "Yeah, Jack. The kid's all right. I think we have an understanding now."

After dinner, Jack tells me we're going to a temple tonight. When I give him a look, he tells me there's a fair. A carnival. The kids want to go, he says. They've been talking about it all month. The girl's starting to catch some of the conversations between Jack and me. She looks at us while we talk and says, "We have fun, Grandfather. We have good time," and I say, "All right, girl. Let's go. I suppose I wouldn't mind whupping you at Skee-Ball."

"Skee-Ball?" the girl asks.

"They don't have Skee-Ball here," Jack informs me.

"Too bad for you," I say to the girl. "Your life's diminished."

She gives her father a confused look. Jack puts a hand on her head, says something to her in Thai, and she bounds up the stairs to get dressed.

"Hey," Jack says to me as I'm watching the girl. "You're smiling, old man. Don't tell me you're in a good mood."

"Jack," I say. "You're pissing me off."

The temple isn't far; it takes only fifteen minutes. The wife helps me out of the car. After she straps me in, she takes a finger from my dead hand and scratches her own face with it. Everybody thinks it's a gas. The kids laugh, Jack laughs, and the wife's so happy with herself tears stream down her face. She's still holding my dead hand and I can almost feel it shaking with her hilarity.

"Ha ha," I say. "Very funny. Now give me my damn hand back."

There's bright lights and loud music and people all over the temple grounds. The boy's beside himself with excitement. He races ahead with his sister, runs back to report on what he's seen. Jack and his wife nod absentmindedly and the kid sprints to join his sister at the gates once more.

"Somebody give that kid a tranquilizer," I say. "He's gonna poop his pants if he doesn't calm down."

It's the usual carny fare. A Ferris wheel, a carousel, giant teacups, a Tilt-A-Whirl, a mini–roller coaster speeding through some poorly conceived jungle scene. All sorts of games and stuffed animals. The temple's monks sit in booths collecting tickets, ruffling their saffron robes every so often like orange birds preening themselves. Thai music blares from the temple's staticky speakers. There's some clown walking around on stilts. He's poking people with a giant foam noodle, laughing and guffawing loudly, his stilts clopping on the pavement like hooves. He's walking toward us now and I'm thinking that if he so much as grazes me with that noodle I'm gonna kick the goddamn stilts from under him. The children are excited. They approach the clown, peer stupidly up at his face. He whacks my grandson on the head a few times. The boy's practically epileptic with delight. When the clown approaches me I give him my best snarl. He seems to get the point. I can almost see the man's smile disappearing beneath that coat of ridiculous clown paint. He quickly diverts his attention to a group of teenage girls nearby.

For a while, we just let the kids lead us through the fair. We stand by the rails and watch them take a few rides. At the Ferris wheel, I can hear my mongrel grandchildren yelling down at us from the sky. The boy waves every time their car dips to its lowest point. One time, the boy screams "ass" over and over again as he's coming down. I laugh. Jack gives me a look. "Nice, Father," he says.

"I didn't teach him that," I say. "Why would I teach him that?"

The girl sees a group of her girlfriends from school. I can tell that she wants to wander the fair with them. She asks Jack and he looks over at his wife. Tida shrugs like she can't see any harm in it. The little boy wants to go with his sister. Jack and Tida are talking to them both now. They have stern, parental looks on their faces. They're telling the girl to take care of her brother. Jack takes off his watch and gives it to my granddaughter. We're to meet back at the Ferris wheel in an hour. Before we can even say good-bye they've joined the crowd snaking their way through the temple grounds.

The three of us wander over to a tent outside the temple gates. Most of the adults have congregated there. There's an empty dance floor with a mirror ball. They're serving beer. I ask Jack to get me one. "I don't know if a man in your condition should be drinking," Jack says, and I say, "Don't be stupid, Jack. My condition's the *reason* a man like me should be drinking." I tell Jack I want a Budweiser and he looks at me like I have horns.

He comes back with a beer for each of us. I'm concentrating hard, trying not to spill it on myself, the liquid dancing against the lip of the plastic cup. Jack asks me if I need help, but I tell him I still know how to drink a beer, thank you very much. Then I spill a little on my lap.

"Dammit," I say.

The wife laughs. Jack smiles and takes the cup from my shaking left hand. "I'll get you a straw," he says. "Dammit," I say again. "Don't get me a straw, Jack. Nobody drinks beer with a straw."

"You need a straw," he says.

A little later Jack tells me his wife wants to dance.

"Go," I say. "Dance. You're a grown man, Jack. You don't need my permission. I'll just sit here and play with my sippee cup."

Jack leads Tida to the dance floor. They're the only people out there. It seems the whole place is watching them. Everybody looks up to watch my son—this tall, foreign man— dancing with his Thai wife. It's a slow Thai song and another couple, both Thai, join them on the floor, the lights from the mirror ball sweeping back and forth. Jack's holding his wife close. They're smiling at each other like there's so much love between them they don't know what to do with it. I'm a little embarrassed; I don't really want to look, though I also can't take my eyes off them. I'm sucking on my beer, thinking how you never get used to seeing your child's romantic side, when I look around and see some of the men under the tent snickering in Jack's direction. I notice, too, that the women are talking to one another sternly, peering at Jack and his wife. I can tell by the way they look at her that they think Tida's some kind of prostitute and suddenly I'm proud of them both for being out there dancing, proud of my boy Jack for holding his wife so close, because their love suddenly seems for the first time like something courageous and worthwhile, and I'm thinking: *There he is, Alice. There's your boy. There's our little man.*

*   *   *

When we meet the kids back at the Ferris wheel, the temple's starting to empty. Some of the monks are sweeping the grounds. My grandkids are talking a mile a minute to Jack and Tida, telling them about all the things they've done. The boy shows me a ratty stuffed giraffe he's won at some game. "How do you do?" he says. He holds the thing proudly above his head. "Gee-raahf!" he says, and I say, "Yeah, kid. Giraffe."

"Grandfather okay?" the girl asks. There's a purple rose painted on each of her cheeks. "Grandfather have fun at temple?"

"Sure," I tell her. "Grandfather had fun. Grandfather drank some beer. Grandfather got a little drunk." The girl looks at me perplexed. Jack and his wife laugh. My son translates for the girl and she grins mischievously at me. "I see," she says, nodding earnestly. "Drunk."

We're halfway out of the temple when I see four teenage boys in bumper cars ramming into each other, giggling like hyenas. My grandson runs up to the rails and watches the boys in there for a while, hugging the giraffe close to his chest.

"Look at that, Jack," I say. "He's just like you. Remember how you used to love bumper cars?"

"Yeah," Jack says. "Sure."

The boy wants to ride the bumper cars. He wants to get in there with the older boys. Jack and his wife both shake their heads no. "C'mon," I say. "Don't be such a curmudgeon."

Jack peers down at me like I amuse him. He says something to the wife, who shrugs, and then he calls his son over.

The boy skips excitedly back to his father. The girl's excited now too. She wants to get in there as well.

The bumper cars come to a sudden stop; time's up for the teenage boys. They all get out, walk over to the monk manning the lever, hand him more money, and return to their cars again, broad smiles on their faces. The monk looks over at Jack and the kids. Jack fishes out his wallet, gives the boy and girl some money.

"We should all go," I say suddenly.

Jack looks at me like I just farted.

"Very funny," he says, watching the kids run over to the monk.

"C'mon, Jack," I say. "It'll be a blast."

"You can't get in there, Father."

"Sure I can."

"Don't be ridiculous."

"Let me get in there with them," I say. "Let me have a little fun with my grandkids."

Before Jack can respond, I'm already waving my good left arm for the monk to hold on, wheeling myself toward the bumper cars. Jack's saying "Father," but I've got the chair on FASTEST, the wheels skipping quickly over the dirt. He and his wife are both walking briskly beside me now, trying to keep up. "Mister Perry," Tida says.

When I get to him, the monk looks down at me, looks up at Jack, looks back at me once more, a wry smile on his face. He pulls his orange robes tighter around him. I wonder for a moment if he's wearing anything under there.

"Give me some money," I say to Jack, holding out my good left hand.

"No," Jack says. "You can't go in there, Father."

"Who says?"

"*He* says." Jack nods in the monk's direction. I peer up at the guy.

"You really say that?" I ask the monk, but the guy just looks at Jack and Tida for help. He says something in Thai and Tida responds, laughing awkwardly. The monk's smiling some more at me now. I look over and see my grandson pretending to drive the bumper car even though it can't go anywhere yet.

"Let me get in there," I say to the monk, nodding in the direction of the cars. "I'll be all right, Mister Monk."

"Father—"

"Jack," I say, turning to my son. "*Please*." But Jack just frowns at me, blinking. "You really want me to be happy here?" I say. "Well, Jack, this is it. This'll make me happy. I swear. You let me in there and I'll be as happy as you want me to be."

Jack licks his lips. I can tell he's thinking about it. I can tell I've almost got him. All the kids stare at us impatiently from their bumper cars. Jack sighs and says something to the monk. The monk just shrugs his shoulders, retrieves a pack of cigarettes from his robes.

"This isn't happening," Jack says, reaching for his wallet.

When Jack gets me out of the wheelchair and carries me across the tarmac, all the kids fall silent. He helps me into an old red car, slides me into the passenger seat. He moves to get in beside me. I tell him to get his own car.

"I'm driving," I say, pulling myself over to the driver seat, dragging my dead right arm along. "That's the damned point, Jack."

"Jesus," Jack says, rolling his eyes, but I just give him this steely look so he walks over to his son's car a few feet away and sits down beside him. I hear a few of the teenagers sniggering. Tida's seated snugly with her daughter across the pit. She's talking about me; the girl nods silently and looks my way every so often.

I've positioned myself comfortably now, the safety belt across my lap, my left foot firm on the acceleration pedal, my good hand a tight fist around the top of the metal steering wheel. The hand feels good. It's remarkably still. I stare at it astonished, like I'm discovering my hand for the very first time.

"C'mon, Mister Monk," I start saying, and as if on cue the mirror ball above us comes to life, music starts blaring through the speakers, sparks start raining down from the electric ceiling, and the car's suddenly like some rocket yanking me through the stratosphere, screeching like a banshee, whipping my whole body around. The kids squeal. I'm laughing hysterically, like somebody's tickling me. I'm laughing and I can't stop. For the first few seconds, I'm not even steering, I'm just laughing and loving the speed of the thing.

My car runs right into the edge of the tarmac. My head whips forward, jerks back quickly, and now I'm laughing even more from the impact. I'm drooling, spittle's flying everywhere, but I don't care about that anymore. I use the heel of my good left hand to steer away from the edge. I look around. I notice that all the kids have steered clear of me. So I start moving toward the pack in the center of the pit.

I see Jack and his son nudging one of the teenagers from behind, the cars bouncing off each other like pool balls. I'm bearing down on them now. I'm gathering speed. I'm a stone flying out of a goddamn slingshot. And then I get them good. I hit Jack and the kid so hard from behind both their heads start bobbing like one of those stupid dolls Mac loved to put on his dashboard. The little boy starts giggling and I'm screaming through the laughter, saying, "Gotcha, gotcha, gotcha, gotcha, gotcha!"

Jack looks at me like I've gone mad, his eyes wide and incredulous, but I just whip the car back around, still using the heel of my palm to steer, and I'm trying to find the wife and her daughter now. I see that they've been cornered by two of the teenagers, so I move over to the side of the pit and wait for an opening. When I see one, I charge through like some running back barreling across a goal line. Just as I'm about to hit them, I swing around to sideswipe, bumping into them even harder than I'd bumped into Jack and the boy. I'm about to ask the girl who's kicking whose ass now but somebody smacks me from the back and when I turn around I see that it's Jack and the boy. I get out of the way and they barrel into Tida and the girl. I see them all laughing now, facing one another in their cars, and I'm circling them, planning my next line of attack. I'm going for the knockout punch, I'm aiming my car directly at both their bumpers, and when we all hit the impact nearly lifts me out of my seat, stretching the seat belt around my waist.

A few more maneuvers and the mirror ball's off, the pit's dark again, there's no more music except our laughing in our bumper cars. I'm soaked in my own sweat. I'm out of breath. I'm gasping for air. There's an awful cramp in my neck. My ass is sore as hell and my hand is purple from gripping the wheel so hard. I'm shaking with adrenaline. I can feel the blood sloshing back and forth through my head. My lips are numb when I wipe at the drool. I watch the teenage boys race out of the pit. I try to get out by myself. I unbuckle the seat belt and start hoisting myself with my good left hand. I nearly slip. But suddenly Jack's right there to help me. He's gripping my quivering body. He's sliding me out of the car and into his arms. "Father?" he asks in a serious voice while I lie there limp in his arms not saying a thing, staring unblinkingly up into his face, and I say, "Shut your trap, boy. Just be quiet. I'm still alive."

COCKFIGHTER

I

Papa kept losing with his cocks. He'd bring them home every Sunday evening quivering inside their traveling coops in the Mazda flatbed, beady little eyes wild with chicken-terror, bold brilliant feathers wet with their own blood. Mama and I would pluck the dead ones. We'd blanch them. We'd bleed them for sausages, feed entrails to the strays. And then we'd roast them because, after all, as Papa would often tell me, a chicken was still a chicken no matter if it's raised to lay eggs or crow at the sun or fight like a gladiator.

I knew it broke Papa's heart to kill those chickens, though. The way he ate his dinner—picking each bone clean, licking his lips and fingers—you'd think he was trying to teach me something about indifference. I, too, tried to make a show of eating, put on my bravest face, for in those days we were nothing if not a family of brave, ridiculous faces. But I wasn't a fool. I knew Papa loved those chickens. At night, I would often hear ululations coming from the ramshackle chicken house, Papa's lantern casting erratic patterns across my bedroom wall. He'd be out there cooing to his chickens for hours.

I didn't know if he was praying or cursing or singing the chickens a lullaby, but for some reason I could never sleep until my father was inside the house, until that light moved from my window and there seemed nothing to the night but the strays howling among the rubber trees at the edge of our property.

Good night, chickens. Good night, Papa.

Then Papa started sleeping with his chickens. For my part, I began to learn how unbearable the night could be. I'd watch my bedroom wall for hours, the shifting shapes of the lantern's glow filling me with dread. My terrors were no longer childish. I saw lewd, horrible men dancing on my walls with fangs, claws, raw red penises. I saw myself naked before them like a slab of meat quivering on a butcher's block. I felt fingernails sinking into my breasts, rancid breath moistening my face, woolly hairs chafing my stomach. Exhaustion invariably took me, but sleep was hardly a relief. I dreamt of sex and I dreamt of decapitations and these dreams were often one and the same.

Mama and I would find Papa in the morning snoring in a bed of straw, a ring of cigarette butts scattered beside him, the cocks clucking for their morning feed. She'd nudge him with her foot. He'd open his eyes suddenly, as if he hadn't been sleeping at all, and then silently go about his business—drizzling feed into the coops, changing water pans, stalking back to the house to take his morning bath—as if it was the most natural thing in the world for a grown man to be caught sleeping with his chickens.

People started to talk. They started to laugh. He'd become a bone for the rumormongers to gnaw. In town, the men would cluck at me, flap their elbows, and I never knew if they were making fun of Papa or making a pass at me or some strange combination of both.

"Your father's losing it," Mama said one morning while we were doing the day's wash out back, up to our elbows in suds. We could hear Papa chasing the chickens through the yard for exercise, their clucks and squawks joining the chorus of early morning birds. During the week, when he wasn't training his chickens, Papa worked at the roofing factory hammering gigantic sheets of tin. "Chickens. Money. His feeble mind. He's losing it all." I nodded, wringing a pair of my father's workpants over the washbasin.

"And your breasts," Mama sighed suddenly, reaching out with a wet hand. "My God, you're getting huge."

"Mama," I muttered, swatting at her fingers. "Don't be disgusting."

"Don't be such a prude," Mama said. "I'm your mother. I gave you those things."

"Mama!"

"Are you pregnant? That would be the end, Ladda. I'd shoot myself if some yahoo knocked you up."

I just kept wringing my father's pants over the washbasin, listening to the chickens squawking and flapping in the yard.

We'd seen better times. Papa used to win. He used to be the best cockfighter in town. The men used to say Papa could cast magic spells that sent his cocks into a bloodthirsty rage. Magic or no, I loved the way Papa would saunter into the house after a day at the cockpit: beaming, large, awesome with pride. He'd plop a wad of cash on the dinner table and Mama would squeal with delight. He'd let me count the money; I'd lick my fingers, judiciously flip through the bills, the way I'd seen gamblers in town fondling their cash after an evening tossing dice. We weren't wealthy but, for a little while, we could buy things. A brand-new bicycle for me. An electric stove for Mama. Orchids for her garden. The Mazda for Papa. A bigger, better television.

But all that changed the day Little Jui showed up at the cockpit.

II

Sixteen years old, heir to Big Jui's fortune and power, Little Jui was as notorious for being his father's son as he was for his methamphetamine habit. He arrived at the cockpit with his bodyguards, his mind infected with the drug-addled delusion that he was no longer a young man attending a cockfight but that he was, in fact, a mangy rabid dog. He got down on all fours. He barked at the chickens. Some say he foamed at the mouth, scratched his ears with his legs, sniffed the men's crotches. At first, nobody paid him any mind, but then some of the men picked up their coops and went home.

To make trouble with Little Jui was to make trouble with Big Jui was to offer yourself up for unfathomable cruelties. In middle school, Little Jui had picked a fight with Samat, the bartender's skinny son, who—unaware as the young often are of the world's lunatic ways—decided to teach Little Jui a thing or two about schoolyard kickboxing. Big Jui caught wind of the matter and we all watched in horror the next day as Little Jui led a beaten Samat through town by a leash tied to his tiny, hairless penis. There was nothing any of us could do about it.

At the cockpit, snapping occasionally out of his methamphetamine dream, Little Jui kept betting against Papa's cocks. Little Jui kept losing. He howled with escalating rage every time another chicken left the pit with a ruptured breast, a gouged eye, a severed wing. His bodyguards, Dam and Dang—two fat, betel-chewing men—handed Papa his money with stone-faced courtesy.

Papa made six thousand baht in four matches from Little Jui alone.

That's when Papa should've quit. He should've known better. He'd always said there was nothing so important as good manners when other people's money starts going into your wallet. The gracious cockfighter, he used to tell me, always spares his opponent needless embarrassment and financial ruin. But Papa must've been thinking of what they did to Samat—how a thing like that could ruin a little boy forever—

and he must've also been thinking of all the other people who'd suffered from the senseless abuse of Little Jui's family through the years. So Papa kept his cocks in the pit. He kept accepting more challenges. He kept taking Little Jui's money.

The men knew Papa had abandoned his customary cockfighting manners for higher stakes. No one in our town had ever defied Little Jui's family. And while this was just a cockfight, there seemed something gratifying about Little Jui losing and losing and losing again, howling like a wounded animal, while Papa's wad of money thickened with every match. And though the men knew better than to cheer, they couldn't suppress their sly, satisfied grins.

It got dark. The cocks had become gray shadows flapping in the night. Papa'd made nine thousand from Little Jui now—the most he'd ever made in an afternoon. The boy was enraged. He threatened to have his bodyguards cripple anyone caught smiling at his defeats. More men went home. Papa decided to do the same. He'd done enough, he thought. No use being reckless.

"Dinnertime," Papa announced ceremoniously, picking up a few coops to take to the Mazda.

"You're not going anywhere," Little Jui cried, a finger pointed at Papa. Dam and Dang moved quickly to Papa's side, thick hands reaching for his arm. "One more, old man. Double or nothing this time."

The pit fell silent. Nobody in our town had ever wagered so much. Papa considered for a moment, blinked at Little Jui.

He opened his mouth to say something, but Little Jui suddenly fell to his hands and knees, rolled around in the dirt, and began to whimper like a dog again. There must've been something about seeing Big Jui's son groveling like that. There must've also been something about having Dam's and Dang's thick fingers wrapped around his skinny forearms. Something, too, about the way the men looked to him now, like he was a hero, like they were pinning unnameable hopes on Papa and his chickens. And there must've been something about the money that stood to be won now—another nine thousand—more than Mama made the whole season sewing fake pearls onto brassieres at home for Miss Mayuree and the lingerie company.

Pack it up, Papa. Leave. Bring those chickens home.

But Papa stayed. He began to prepare Somsak, a meter-tall Thai bantam he'd named after his own father, my grandfather. Papa rarely fought Somsak. He'd only bring the cock out for big matches. With his vermilion breast and his green crown set against a canvas of iridescent indigo feathers, Somsak was once named "Native Chicken of the Week" by one of the cockfighting magazines. We had the spread pinned to the refrigerator door. Pictures of Papa handling the cock. Somsak leaping, midair, a dazzling swirl of colors. Complex diagrams of the chicken's imperial plumage. Somsak never lost, though he'd been close once, when an opposing chicken's spur punctured one of his lungs. Between rounds, Papa inserted a straw through the wound and sucked out the blood filling the chicken's chest cavity. Somsak reentered the pit energetic as ever. He won the match. Later that evening Papa sutured the wound with Mama's sewing kit while I held the quivering chicken between my knees. The next morning Somsak was out there dashing and flapping across the yard with the rest of the chicken house.

The rumormongers used to say Somsak's name was no accident. He was my grandfather's spirit reincarnated in poultry form, back to give Papa what my grandfather couldn't give in life. Which might not be so silly, because Papa always said the real Somsak never gave him anything but bruised buttocks and a broken home.

While Papa prepared Somsak—slicking the cock's feathers, attaching the spur to his leg, pinching his purple gullet—Little Jui tried to find a suitable opponent, walked around the pit examining the other men's chickens. Ignorant of the pit's standards, he chose an aging, diseased rooster long past its prime, a creature so fat the men called it The Hen. The owner tried to convince Little Jui that The Hen didn't stand a chance. It wasn't going to be a match, he warned Little Jui, it was going to be a slaughter. But Little Jui said he knew they were all conspiring against him, that they wanted to see him lose, so shut the fuck up, I know a good chicken when I see one, I mean just look at the fat fuck, he's a goddamn ostrich, he's the motherfucking emperor of chickens, so get him ready or I'll show you a slaughter, I'll have my bodyguards stuff that chicken's bulbous head up your tiny little asshole.

The men sized up the cocks, beaked them in the center of the pit. Somsak thrashed and bucked violently in Papa's hands. The Hen, in the meantime, dashed toward the pit perimeter, which sent all the men scurrying because—like Papa always said—when a gamecock gets loose and flaps around with its spur you'd better get out of the way, lest you get stabbed by the errant chicken. But The Hen wasn't the nimblest of creatures. His owner managed to retrieve him before anybody got hurt.

Order was restored. The men beaked the chickens again to agitate them anew. The cocks were released. Somsak leapt into the air and—with the first blow—swung his gaff-blade directly into The Hen's neck. The men said later that you'd think Somsak was the chicken Bruce Lee, it was that beautiful. The Hen crumpled immediately, like a deflated feather balloon. He'd nearly been beheaded. The pit silt turned red with The Hen's blood.

Game over. Papa wins again.

But before Papa could retrieve Somsak—who now strutted around The Hen like a boxer taunting his collapsed opponent—Little Jui shrieked and leapt over the pit fence. All the men stood stupefied as the boy wrestled my grandfather's namesake to the ground. He pinned the squawking cock beneath his knees. He bent down, stuffed the cock's crown into his mouth. He bit off Somsak's head.

And then Little Jui just sat there with his mouth full of feathers, blood dribbling down his chin, a crazed, petulant grin on his face, before spitting Somsak's head in Papa's direction.

"Draw," he declared triumphantly. "Nobody wins."

Papa picked up Somsak's head and threw it back at Little Jui.

"You barbarian," he screamed. "You animal." Papa moved toward the cockpit, but Little Jui's bodyguards quickly wrestled him to the ground. You'd think Little Jui was the prime minister and Papa some crazed assassin the way those bodyguards descended upon my father. One of them sat on his chest, pinned Papa's arms with his fists. The other put a handgun to Papa's head.

Little Jui started laughing then, high-pitched, deranged, still straddling Somsak. The rumormongers said later that as Little Jui sat there laughing, Somsak's headless body flapped its wings for the final time. There seemed something strange about the scenario then, how Papa had gone so quickly from being a hero among heroes to having both his body and his prized chicken, now headless, pinned to the earth.

"Aw," Little Jui said. "Don't cry, old man. It was just a chicken." Papa tried to speak, but with the bodyguard's weight on his chest he could only gasp for air. Little Jui crawled toward Papa. He hung his head over my father's purpling grimace.

"You know," he whispered, smiling, blood dripping from his chin onto Papa's cheeks, "I could kill you, old man. All Dam has to do is squeeze." Papa stared up at Little Jui, squeaking, still trying to speak. Dam dug the gun's muzzle into the side of Papa's head.

"Stop it," one of the men said.

"There's no need for this," said another man.

"It's just like you said, Little Jui. Nobody wins."

"That's right, Little Jui. It's a draw. It's always a draw when both chickens die."

But Little Jui just kept on panting into my father's anguished face. He spat into my father's eyes.

"All right," he said to Dam and Dang, standing now, wiping his lips with a forearm. "Get off the geezer."

They let Papa go. Little Jui walked away from the pit with his bodyguards, back down the dirt road that led to the town's main avenue. The men gathered around my father, asked if he was all right, but Papa just lay there gazing at the night sky as if struck dumb by the stars.

"If you were a man," Papa yelled suddenly, before Little Jui disappeared around the bend, and for a second the men could not tell if my father was chastising the heavens or addressing Big Jui's son. Little Jui stopped and turned to face my father.

"If you were a man," Papa yelled again, getting to his feet, pointing a finger at Little Jui, "you'd at least fight with your own chickens."

"Don't be ungrateful, old man," Little Jui yelled back. "Don't make Dam finish what he started."

"You should've killed me when you could, you ingrate," Papa said. "It's shameful what you just did."

"Keep talking, old man. Keep talking and we'll see—"

"We'll see what, Little Jui? We'll see what a man you are? We'll see if you can beat me up with your overweight goons?" Papa spat in Little Jui's direction. Some of the men grabbed Papa, urged him to relent. "That's what you are," Papa continued, pointing at the patch of ground he'd just spat on. "You're nothing but a piece of phlegm walking the face of the earth."

"Watch it, old man. I'd be very careful—"

"Who do you think you are, you son-of-a-bitch? Who do you think you are that you can bite my chicken's head off like that? Everybody knows I won fair and square. You think you're a man, Little Jui? A man?" Papa stalked slowly down the dirt road toward Little Jui, jabbing his finger in the boy's direction. "A man? Ha! I'll tell you what you are, Little Jui. You're not a man. You're an animal. A beast. My chickens have more decency and self-respect than you and your kind."

"Keep going, old man. Keep it up. See where it gets you."

"You'll die one day, Little Jui," Papa continued. "And when you die you'll wonder why you wasted your life the way you did. You'll die wondering if people love you for who you are or because they fear your father. If anyone, in fact, ever really loved you at all, and—"

"I'm warning you, old man," Little Jui said coolly. "Enough with the public-service announcement."

But Papa just kept on walking toward Little Jui, yelling at the boy. Though the men were afraid for my father, though they wanted to stop his ranting down that dark dirt road, they also couldn't bring themselves to call out to him. For something strange seemed to be happening now. Little Jui was cowering angrily before my father. Papa's words seemed to diminish the boy.

Then Little Jui grabbed the gun from Dam's hip. He fired a shot into the night. Like lightning, the firearm's flash revealed Papa and Little Jui and his bodyguards frozen in their respective poses: Papa with his finger in Little Jui's face, the handgun in Little Jui's right fist pointed clumsily to the sky, Dam and Dang looking bewildered beside them both. The scent of gunpowder filled the air. Animals scuttled in the underbrush. The cocks flapped in panicked staccatos. Many of the men yelped. Some instinctively fell for cover. But Papa just stood his ground—finger in the air, mouth opened, body mid-stride. The shot had silenced him. The seconds stretched interminably. The men held their breaths. Little Jui pressed the muzzle of the gun against my father's forehead. Papa flinched from the iron's heat. When he came home later that evening, there would be a small, dark ring of swollen flesh protruding like some strange Hindu emblem from the middle of his forehead.

"Don't be stupid," Little Jui hissed. "Don't push it, old man."

Then Little Jui raised the pistol high into the air and brought it down upon the side of my father's face. Papa fell to the ground. As Papa braced himself, Dam and Dang descended upon him with a flurry of indiscriminate kicks, like two fat children clumsily vying for a football.

"Know your place," Little Jui said, when Dam and Dang had exhausted themselves. And then they walked away, their shadows disappearing down the dirt road as Papa lay there heaving.

Later that night, from my bedroom window, I watched Mama tend to Papa's wounds outside. She rubbed ointment into his bruised torso. She swabbed his brow with alcohol. She muttered profanities under her breath. Papa stared blankly out into the rubber trees, wincing every so often, the strays' high-pitched howls echoing in the night.

"You idiot," I heard Mama mutter. "You moron. What did I tell you? This cockfighting business—it's dangerous. Promise me you'll never go back, Wichian. Promise me you'll never fight another chicken so long as you live." But Papa just kept on staring out into the night. Mama began to cry then as she applied a bandage to one of his wounds. Papa reached out with a consoling hand, but Mama recoiled from the gesture. And as I watched my parents bathing in that moonlight, I began to understand for the first time what kind of world we were living in, what men were capable of, and I longed more than anything to take the three of us to someplace safer, far, far away.

III

Later that week, as I biked home from school, Little Jui eased up in his Range Rover beside me, arms and head hanging limply out the back window, the engine growling like some awful mechanical beast. Dam was driving the car; Dang prodded a zit in the mirror of the passenger-seat visor. I could smell the sour scent of cologne and nicotine and alcohol wafting from Little Jui's head. I kept on biking, concentrating on the road ahead.

"Oooh, girl," he cooed. "Why don't you throw your bike in the trunk. Why don't we go for a ride. You're making me hard." I tried to pedal faster. But the faster I went, the closer that Range Rover seemed to draw up beside me.

"What's the rush?" He glowered at me, smiled lazily. "Don't be scared," he said. "Little Jui won't hurt you. Little Jui just wants to show you a thing or two."

"Go away," I muttered.

"Don't be that way," he said, laughing. "I've seen the way you look at me, girl. I've been watching you. We're not children anymore, you know. Just think about the things we could do. We could touch tongues. We could fondle each other. We could do it doggie-style."

"Leave me alone."

"Did I ever tell you how much I love your breasts? I love 'em, Ladda. I was just telling Dam and Dang about them the other day. Hey, guys"—Little Jui leaned forward in his seat, tapped Dam's and Dang's shoulders—"wasn't I just telling you about her boobies?" The bodyguards looked over briefly. They chuckled. One of them winked at me. "See? I dream about your breasts, girl," Little Jui continued. "I think about them all the time. I imagine them jiggling when I spank my little monkey at night."

I stood up on my bike, pumping furiously now at the pedals. I managed to pull ahead of their car, but the Range Rover caught up with me again, Little Jui's face leering out the window like the head of some aberrant dog enjoying an afternoon car ride. In the distance, I saw Papa's figure in the yard, still dressed in his gray factory uniform, feeding the chickens. Mama was working at her lingerie on the front porch.

"There's your old man," Little Jui said, following my gaze. "How's he doing these days?"

"Leave my father alone. He never did anything to you."

"Say hi for me," he said. "Tell him I'll be back at the pit on Sunday. And tell him"—Little Jui leaned far out of the car now, almost whispering into my ear—"tell him I'm going to fuck his daughter one of these days." He puckered his lips, made sucking noises at me, and then they sped away. They honked when they passed the house, long obnoxious bleats echoing down the road, and through that thick dirt cloud Little

Jui yelled something toward my parents. Mama leapt to her feet, ran screaming toward them, but by the time she got to the road the Range Rover was far out of sight.

When I arrived at the house, Mama was out in the yard yelling at Papa, gesticulating wildly with her hands.

"You can't be serious," she cried. "You can't go back, Wichian."

"Don't be hysterical," Papa said, smiling at me through swollen eyes, his face still bruised, the chickens waddling around his feet. I knew I should tell them about my encounter with Little Jui, but instead I just stared at the welt on Papa's forehead, wondering how he could stand there grinning when he'd been pistol-whipped just a few days ago.

"'Hysterical'?" Mama cried. "Don't you remember what they did to you? You want to die? Is that it, Wichian? You want to make me a widow?"

"Don't be so dramatic. You never complained when I was bringing money home from the pit." Papa bent down to stroke one of the chickens. "You never complained when I was buying your orchids and your electric stove."

"But this is different, Wichian," Mama said. "You know this is different."

"If I don't show up at the pit, then it means they've scared us," Papa said, crouching now. "It means they've won. I refuse to give them that satisfaction, Saiya. Besides," Papa continued, "what else am I supposed to do with these chickens?"

"Fuck the chickens," Mama yelled, kicking at the creatures. The cocks lurched into the air before settling nervously back on the ground.

"Hey. Watch it. Chickens are delicate animals."

"You want to be a hero?" Mama yelled, ignoring him. "You want to be the good guy? This isn't a movie, Wichian. There are no good guys. And even if there were, even if this was a movie, I've seen this one before. This is the one where the good guy dies and his family ends up with nothing but a bunch of useless chickens squawking in the yard to remind them of his stupidity."

IV

Word got around town that Little Jui would bring cocks of his own to the pit that Sunday. He'd procured, with his father's help, four Filipino purebreds and a prodigal eighteen-year-old handler from Manila named Ramon. Rumors had it that Ramon—who was seen accompanying Little Jui in town that week—could hypnotize his chickens. He'd meditate with them every morning to synchronize their auras. During a match, Ramon would murmur to the cocks, urge them on in a language that the chickens understood but that sounded strange and inhuman to everybody else. According to the men, Ramon had once trained a plump, egg-laying hen for the world-famous Manila pits and won.

"Men are lunatics, Ladda." Mama sighed. She was behind schedule with the bras again; I was helping her pin ornate lace trims to foam cups. The lingerie company demanded eight hundred finished bras a month. We needed to make three hundred more in seven days. Papa was still at the factory hammering tin. "You'd think God invented stupidity the same day he came up with the penis."

"What are you talking about, Mama?"

"Don't act dumb, girl. I'm talking about the fuss these men make over their stupid chickens." Mama bit off a piece of thread, spat the tendrils out between her teeth. "Meditating with their chickens. Ha!"

"Cockfighting is an ancient tradition, Mama," I said, throwing a finished piece onto the large heap between us. "It's the sport of kings. You know, King Naresuan was a champion cockfighter during his reign."

"Don't start, Ladda."

"It's true. I even looked it up at the library to make sure Papa wasn't lying."

"Even if that was true," Mama said, putting down the bra she was working on, "don't forget that Mister Cockfighting King got killed riding an elephant into battle." She tapped her head with a finger.

I got up to stretch my limbs; I didn't want to talk about it anymore.

"I don't want your father going back to that cockpit," Mama said. "Not after what they did to him. He acts like he hasn't been living here all his life. Talk to your father, will you? Maybe he'll listen to you."

I nodded, sat back down.

"He doesn't know what he's getting into," Mama continued. I nodded again, tried to concentrate on the work at hand.

"Try this," Mama said suddenly, throwing a finished bra in my direction, a red and black contraption studded with dozens of fake pearls. "I think it's your size."

"I don't think so," I said, catching the bra, tossing it back onto the mound between us. "It's hideous, Mama."

"C'mon. It won't bite," Mama said. "It's ugly, I know. But it's underwear. Nobody'll see it. You're fifteen now. Time to stop showing strangers your nipples."

"But you didn't wear a bra until you were thirty, Mama."

"I know," Mama said. "But we didn't have them then. Those were barbarous times, you know. We lived like monkeys. We didn't have television. We didn't have cars. We danced naked around bonfires at night. We wore diapers to catch our menses. You should be thankful for the times, Ladda. Be thankful for this bra. You should be thankful for the modern age."

V

I tried to speak to Papa that Saturday. He was out in the chicken house sharpening his spurs, the whetstone singing a high, insistent note like an asthmatic wheezing in the night. Fireflies winked in the rubber trees. "Hey," he said when I opened the chicken-house door.

I settled onto a bale of straw as Papa sprinkled water from a bowl over the whetstone with his fingers. The whetstone shimmered under the light of the oil lantern at his side. The spurs lay at his feet in a neat, military row, arranged from shortest to longest like toy scythes laid out for some miniature farm auction. All the cocks slept peacefully in their coops, crowns tucked into their pillowy breasts. Papa laid the whetstone down and bent toward the lantern to light a cigarette.

"I know your mother doesn't want me going to the cockpit tomorrow," he said, exhaling ribbons of smoke through his teeth, picking up the whetstone again. The scent of burnt cloves filled the chicken-house air. As Papa spoke, I realized I hadn't seen my father's bruises up close. They looked like splotchy indigo maps.

"She just doesn't want you to get hurt."

"I know," he said. "What do you think I should do, Ladda?"

"Don't go," I said curtly. I was surprised by the directness of my response. My face suddenly swelled with emotion, peering at the bruises on my father's face. "It's not worth it, Papa."

He looked at me. Then he went back to sharpening a spur, the blade glinting as he wiped it back and forth across the whetstone plane. We sat silently for a while. I watched our shadows dance on the mud walls. Outside, the strays started in on their howling.

"Well," Papa said, sliding the spurs into their vellum sheaths. "You might be right, Ladda. It might not be worth it." He put out the cigarette on the soles of his slippers, stowed the spurs into the case Mama had sewed for him years ago. "But," he continued, "living in fear wouldn't be worth it either."

"Papa—"

"It's a scary world, Ladda," Papa said, smiling at me, clicking the case shut. "This isn't a matter of honor, Ladda. It isn't even about standing up to Little Jui and his kind. It's about choosing whether you're going to let the world run you ragged and scared or whether you're going to say to the world: 'Hey, World. Hey, asshole. Yeah, you. That's right, I'm talking to you. I know you're scary but you know what, World? I refuse to run. I refuse to let you push me around. I, Wichian, am staying right where I am.'"

I couldn't help but laugh then, imagining Papa confronting a giant cartoon globe with stubby little legs. My father joined in. We sat there laughing in that chicken house for a bit. I got up, brushed the straw from the seat of my pants. "Hey," he said. "When did you start wearing a bra?"

"What's with you people?" I said exasperatedly, walking toward the door. "Leave me alone."

VI

So Papa went back to the pit. That Sunday afternoon, while he was away, Mama and I sat on the porch sewing the last of the month's quota, packing the bras into cardboard shipping boxes. Miss Mayuree, the company's representative, was coming to pick up the bras the next day. We worked silently, furiously, the sun arcing slowly across the sky. Mama didn't say much. She was worried about Papa. She jolted a little every time a car engine could be heard rumbling down the road. I tried to make small talk. I told her stories about high school: the drunken math teacher, the schoolyard courtships, the latest rumors and intrigues. I even ventured a few jokes about the leather-tasseled novelty models we'd made, but Mama smiled at me as if to say, *Thanks for the effort, little daughter, but let's just finish these bras. Let's hope your father makes it home tonight.*

The sun began to set. Mama was worried now. She furrowed her brow. She shook her legs involuntarily. She went into the house and came out with Papa's flask of Mekong. Mama drank when she was nervous. She poured a generous dram into the tumbler. She took a few sips and settled onto the porch floor beside me, stuffing bras into plastic bags while I sorted the models and put them in their appropriate boxes. She offered me the tumbler and I, too, took a few sips even though I hated the way the fiery liquid burned.

"I can't stand this," Mama said, swirling the whiskey in its tumbler, looking down the road again.

"Soon, Mama," I said, the whiskey hot and heavy in my stomach. "Don't worry. He's probably having a good day. He's probably winning."

"I don't care about that," Mama said. I didn't know what to say, so I just kept on stacking the bras into their boxes.

"I'll tell you a story," Mama said suddenly, filling the tumbler once more. "Listen up," she said. "Your father had a sister once."

I stopped working, looked at my mother.

"You didn't know that, did you?" She raised her eyebrows conspiratorially. "Well, I suppose there'd be no reason for you to know. Nobody likes to talk about it anymore, not even the ninnies in town.

"This sister," Mama continued. "She was a little slow, if you know what I mean. She was older than your father, too—about thirty, by the time I met her. Your father would come home from the high school and take her into town every afternoon. He'd buy her a bag of iced tea and they'd sit together on one of the park benches playing imaginary games. They'd laugh and guffaw like children. When I first met your father, I thought it was cute how he took care of his sister, even though the other boys made fun of him, kept calling her a tard to his face. But your father paid them no mind. She was his sister. There was nobody else to care for her, with your grandparents being the lunatics they were.

"Your father was different in those days," Mama said, staring blankly into the tumbler. "He wanted to be a pilot—did you know that? He wanted to fly planes. I'd sit with him in the schoolyard during lunch and he wouldn't shut up about jets and flight controls and horsepower. Your father was going to be the Thai Charles Lindbergh. That's what he liked to say. We were going to move to Bangkok. He was going to fly me across the Pacific." Mama chuckled at the idea, swallowed another sip of whiskey. "So when your father went to officer school in Bangkok, there was nobody to take care of his sister."

An engine echoed down the road. Mama stood up to see if it might be Papa. But it was just a farmer puttering by in his tractor. She sat back down on the porch and we watched the tractor's dim shadow moving by the house like some enormous barge inching down a dark river.

"So what happened, Mama?"

"Awful things," Mama said, shaking her head. "Unspeakable things. She started hanging around the teashops. The men thought it was funny at first. They'd make her sing and dance in her unfortunate ways for small change. And she'd be happy about it, too. She didn't know better. I tried to talk to the men. I told them to leave her alone. But it was already too late. The girl was convinced she'd made some new friends.

"Little Jui's father was one of those men. We call him Big Jui now, but back then he was Little Jui as well. He was just a teenager. He started the whole despicable business. One thing led to another. Soon, she wasn't just singing and dancing anymore. I once walked by the teashop and saw your father's sister down on all fours. All the men laughed while

Big Jui sat there patting her head. It made me want to scream."

"My God."

"I didn't have the heart to write to your father about it; I didn't want him to worry over something he couldn't change. So I tried to talk to your grandparents. I came to this very house," Mama said, gesturing with a half-nod around us. "I stood on this porch and told them what the men were doing to their daughter. But your grandmother just called me a slut and told me to mind my own business. You should count your blessings you never got to meet your grandparents, Ladda. Those people were savages."

It was dark now. As my mother talked, I'd managed to pack the rest of the bras without even realizing it. Mama hung her legs over the porch, poured herself another dram. I joined her there and we both looked down the road, waiting for Papa's Mazda.

"Done," I said softly. "The bras are ready to go."

"Good."

"Papa should be home soon," I said. Mama took another sip of her whiskey, stared out into the rubber trees, and it was as if there, in that grove of tall, spindly trunks, was the picture of the past she'd just been conjuring.

"So what happened to Papa's sister?"

"One of the men in the teashop was a doctor," Mama said. "He told Big Jui that—given the way she was—your father's sister was probably sterile."

"No."

"If there's one thing you should know by now, Ladda, it's that men are monsters," Mama said. "They have no decency. The best a woman can do is learn to tolerate one barbaric thing to the next."

Mama looked at me, paused to pour another dram. She held out the tumbler and I took a few more sips before passing it back to her. "Anyhow," she continued, "your father came home for the summer. A week later, he saw his sister and Big Jui in one of the town alleys. He tried to attack Big Jui, but his witless sister just kept on wailing and grunting, telling your father that Big Jui was her man now. They were in love, she said. They were going to get married. Your father tried to drag his sister away, but she refused to leave Big Jui's side. She slapped him. Big Jui started laughing then. Your father told me later it was like hearing the devil's laughter.

"Your father went home, got his father's gun, and started walking back into town, hell-bent on killing Big Jui. His mother tried to talk him out of it, but your father wouldn't listen. She called to tell me and I went biking around town looking for him. I found your father on the main road, halfway to town. He was crying, cradling his father's shotgun like it was a baby. And that," Mama said, turning to look at me severely, "was the only time I've ever seen your father cry.

"He never went back to officer school. He shut himself up in this house. He refused to go into town. That's when he started cockfighting. I rarely saw him those first few months, but I'd see his sister walking around town. She no longer went home. She slept in the park. She was long gone by then. She followed Big Jui wherever he went, cooing and sidling up to him. He started avoiding her and soon she moved on to the other men, tried to fondle them on the street in broad daylight, though people said you could still hear her wailing outside Big Jui's window every night. Later that year, she was found dead of malnutrition on one of the park benches."

Mama got up, teetering a bit, and started walking back to the house to put the whiskey away. As she stood in the doorway, holding the tumbler and the flask, she turned to me and said:

"I suppose she was your aunt, Ladda. I guess that's why I'm telling you all this. I don't know what difference it makes, though. I hadn't thought about that girl for so long, but I've thought about her a lot lately. Can't help but wonder if this cockfighting thing has something to do with her. Even if your father refuses to admit it. Even if nobody likes to remember her now."

Then Mama went inside the house. I heard her fumbling in the kitchen, the water hissing in the sink, the tumbler clanking against the porcelain basin. I watched the fireflies for a little while. I listened to the strays. Fruit bats circled above the yard. I thought about what my mother had just told me, tried to picture this aunt of mine and her witless love for Big Jui. I got up, put the boxes in order, stacked them neatly against the wall. Just then, far down the road, I saw the Mazda's headlights veer around the bend. For a few seconds, those golden shafts of light cutting through the dark filled me with relief and astonishment, even as I began to feel sick with anguish. And so I yelled out to my mother to say Papa was finally home.

VII

We stood on the porch and watched the Mazda ease into the driveway. Papa's shadow emerged from the car. "See?" he said. "Nothing to be afraid of, Saiya. I'm safe. I'm home." He walked back to the flatbed to gather up the coops. All was fine, far as we could tell. I went to help him. But as I got closer, I noticed Papa staring pensively into the flatbed. Something was wrong. "Hey," Papa said, turning to smile at me. "Did you guys finish the bras?"

"Yeah."

"Good," he replied absentmindedly, staring back into the flatbed.

When I got to the truck, Papa put an arm around my shoulder. I smelled it before I saw anything: chicken blood, sweet and sick and unmistakable. I peered over the edge of the truck and there, in the pit of the flatbed, I saw a mound of dead cocks—a messy heap of feathers and innards and mangled wings piled high against the cab. They seemed like the singular body of some monstrous creature devastated beyond repair. Dull rivulets of blood carved their way along the flatbed. Some of the chickens, I noticed, were still alive; something in the

mound twitched sporadically. I felt then as if that pile of carcasses was winking at me. I wanted to run away. I wanted to
go back to my mother on the porch. But I just stood there
bewitched by that convulsing half-dead pile. Papa tightened
his grip around my shoulder. I wanted to return the embrace
even as I longed to strike him with all my might, for I felt like
Papa was forcing me now with his firm, insistent hold to look
at the carnage.

"I'm sorry, Papa" was all I managed to say. "Sometimes
you win," he said, letting go of my shoulder, bending down to
pick up the surviving chickens. "And sometimes you lose."

"Wichian," Mama said grimly, walking toward us. "What
happened?" But Papa just picked up the coops and walked
toward the chicken house, the surviving cocks shuffling clumsily in their wicker coops. "Hey, cockfighter," Mama called
after him, "what the hell do we do with the dead ones?" But
Papa had already disappeared into the chicken house and we
wouldn't see him again until morning.

Mama saved one for the next day's breakfast, the plumpest
she could find, a creature I recognized by its plumage as Saksri
Bualoi. She picked up Saksri's body, deposited it on the porch
steps, the cock's head swinging by a thin tether of flesh. Saksri
was named after the welterweight champion of the world at
the time, a boy who grew up in a nearby town—the only Thai
world champion of anything, according to Mama. We'd been
watching the real Saksri Bualoi pummel a fat Russian chal-
lenger on television years ago when Papa said that if chickens

had a left hook, the new hatchling he'd just bought was just like Saksri Bualoi, and that's how the cock got its name. But Saksri Bualoi would not be fighting anymore. He would be going into our breakfast now.

We carried the rest of the carcasses to the ditch marking our property. As I carried one, I felt its bloody, slithery neck wriggling in my hand, heard the thing purr like a frightened kitten. I quickly dropped it to the ground and—panicking—kicked it. The cock's body skipped across the yard like a football. Then, to my horror, the chicken got on its feet and ran a few short paces before collapsing dead once and for all.

"It's still got a little juice!" Mama said, laughing. "Don't be scared, Ladda. It can't hurt you now."

But I didn't want to touch it anymore. All I could do was nudge the carcass with my foot, flipping it across the yard, making slow and cautious progress toward the ditch, expecting the thing to get up and run around again. In the distance, I saw Mama toss a couple of carcasses like they were small, feathery sacks of garbage, their bodies thudding in the ditch.

Once we'd transported all the carcasses, Mama went back to the house to get gasoline. We set the pile on fire, then stood silently over the pyre for a while. Blue flames licked up around the carcasses' feathers. Soon, a yellowish inferno danced enthusiastically over the pile, its syncopated pops and crackles echoing down the long corridor of trees before us. Mama poked the pyre with a branch. The fire answered with hisses and cries, the sound of fat smoldering. The air began to smell of burnt chicken-flesh, and I thought of the vendors in town with their street-side fried chicken stalls, fanning themselves with the day's paper, thick sheets of vapor rising from their fryers.

"We'll figure this out in the morning," Mama said softly. We walked back to the house with the pyre still roaring behind us. Mama sat on the porch and picked up Saksri Bualoi. She began to pluck him, snapping fistfuls of feathers from the cock's lifeless body.

That was my first sleepless night: my father in the chicken house, the carcasses burning in the ditch, Mama outside cleaning Saksri Bualoi. I stood by my bedroom window and watched the flames dance until they became nothing but a tiny orange pinprick in the distance.

I thought about what happened to that woman who was my aunt. I thought about Papa crying on the side of the road, cradling his father's shotgun, having only made it halfway to town. I wondered if things would be different now if Papa hadn't lost his will. Would Papa have lessened the sum total of the world's suffering by killing Big Jui? Or would other Juis—Big and Little—have appeared in their place? Would I still love my father knowing he was capable of such violence? Would Mama? Where did murderous vengeance end and principled righteousness—justice—begin? Staring out my bedroom window, I loved Papa for not making it to town that night even as I despised him for losing courage. For it seemed to me that whatever had happened at the cockpit to produce that pyre of chickens might've been averted had Papa not cried like a fucking baby by the side of the road. And as Mama finished cleaning Saksri Bualoi; as I watched the fire die out like some fallen star; as the strays' shadows emerged one by one to inspect that sizzling mess of cremated chicken parts—I wanted more than anything to return to life before Mama had told me her story about Papa's no-name sister. For I felt like Mama had pushed me violently down a one-way street with her cockamamie story, a street I never wanted to go down in the first place. There would be no turning back now, though at the time I couldn't say why or from what.

VIII

Papa had never lost like this. He'd never come home with more than two dead cocks. You can't win every time, that's what he always said; even the expert cockfighter loses once in a while. Nevertheless, losing was one thing; nine dead cocks was another altogether. He'd lost nearly half the chicken house.

The next morning we sat quietly around the kitchen table while Mama dished porridge. Papa hadn't slept much the night before, though it was difficult to distinguish the old bruises on his face from the way his eyelids sagged and swelled. He shuffled in from the chicken house, sat down, and stared out the kitchen window. Tiny chunks of straw clung to his shirt collar. Gray hair sprouted from his head in strange, unruly wisps. Thin wreaths of steam rose from our bowls. Outside, the sun was starting to rise through the trees and I watched a stray—a gaunt, brown puppy with a stunted tail—nose the diminished mess in the ditch.

We started eating. My stomach lurched at the chunks of white meat wedged within the thick of my porridge. I asked Papa what happened. I tried to sound casual. "Nothing," Papa muttered through a mouthful, still staring out the kitchen window. "I lost."

"I'll say," Mama said. She hadn't touched her breakfast yet. She just stared at Papa defiantly, waited for an explanation. Papa shoveled more porridge into his mouth. I stirred my bowl, picked out chunks of chicken and deposited them on the napkin beside me. I thought about the half-dead zombie chicken from the night before, the way it purred in my hand, skittered across the yard when I kicked it. I thought of Saksri Bualoi, his head swinging by a thimble of flesh, the way Mama plucked his feathers by the fistful. I wondered briefly if I had been dreaming the past night's events—they seemed unreal by the light of morning—but those tiny white chunks piled on my napkin told me otherwise.

"How much did you lose, Wichian?" Mama finally asked.

"Eleven thousand," Papa said calmly.

"Oi," Mama cried, throwing up her hands. "Goddammit, Wichian."

"It's that Filipino kid," Papa said, smiling weakly at Mama. "That Ramon. He's good. He knows what he's doing. And you should've seen the Filipino purebreds, Saiya. They're huge. Almost as tall as Ladda here. I didn't think chickens got that big."

"Oi," Mama said again. She shoved her bowl in front of her. It teetered on the linoleum tabletop, porridge dribbling over the lip. "How could you, Wichian?"

"I'll get it back," Papa muttered, turning to his bowl as if there was nothing he'd rather do than watch his porridge cool.

"You'd better," Mama said.

"Well, he made nine thousand last week, Mama," I interjected, but when I looked into Mama's eyes—saw the exasperation there—I regretted saying anything at all. I looked at Papa instead. "So, really, you only lost two thousand, right, Papa?"

"Eat your porridge, Ladda," Mama scoffed.

"Saiya," Papa said.

"How could you lose so much money?" Mama said. But Papa just stared at Mama, biting hard on his bottom lip. Then he got up, dismissed Mama with an impatient half-gesture, and walked out of the kitchen.

"That's right," Mama called after him. "Walk away. Go tend to your fucking chickens."

Then it was just me and Mama staring at one another. My mother seemed the picture of vindictiveness; even as she looked devastated by the eleven thousand lost. "What?" she asked, picking up her porridge bowl. "Stop looking at me like that." But all I managed to say was "It's enough he lost, Mama. Go easy on him."

Papa emerged from the chicken house with the fourteen remaining cocks. We watched him through the kitchen window. He chased them with a different kind of gait that morning. It wasn't the calm, quiet routine we were used to seeing, but a grunting, punishing one. He cursed. He kicked at the dirt. He ran the chickens with what seemed to me like fury, as if the chickens had offended him somehow. Some of the chickens eyed him cautiously, alarmed by his new persona. The sun's red orb rose high above our property; thick beads of perspiration glistened on Papa's forehead.

"Just look at him," Mama said, collecting the bowls, moving to the sink. "Just look at your father, Ladda." I sat there blinking at her. "He's scared," she continued. She turned on the spigot, the water plashing against the bowls. "Your father's terrified."

I went to my room to change for school. Papa put the cocks back in their coops. I watched him carry them one by one to the chicken house, his body slumped and heaving from the run, from their weight. He walked back to the house and soon I could hear him changing into his factory uniform on the other side of the wall. He was still cursing under his breath. He slammed the dresser drawers. I thought I heard him kick something. The sink hissed and clanked in the kitchen, tin utensils ratcheting in the basin. I heard Mama drop a bowl, heard it shatter against the kitchen floor, followed shortly by the swish and tinkle of her sweeping.

And then it was quiet. Mama finished with the dishes. Papa settled down. I inspected myself in the mirror, made sure my uniform was tucked in properly, that the bra's obscene trimmings didn't stand out against the linen. And then, still standing before the mirror, I listened to the sudden silence in our house. I wondered what Papa was doing alone in that room; I listened for any sign of him on the other side of the wall. I wondered, too, what Mama was thinking in the kitchen now. Outside, the brown puppy had left the ditch, the pile already picked over by the larger strays before him.

Mama said Papa was terrified and I wondered if she might be right. I'd never thought of Papa as a terrified man. When he told me that he, Wichian, wasn't going to be scared, I had believed him; those bruises on his face seemed to verify my conviction. But now—in that confounding pause, staring at my own image reflected strangely in the mirror—I began to have my doubts, for I never thought Papa would ever come home with nine dead chickens, never thought he'd lose eleven thousand. I never thought Little Jui and that Filipino boy would beat my father at his own game. And I knew that Papa did not anticipate this either. Things might've been better had he come home instead with a thousand more bruises.

The house came back to life again. Papa slammed the door. He walked out to the Mazda. Mama turned on the radio in the kitchen. I went to get my bicycle. As I stood in the yard strapping my schoolbag to the bike's gridiron backseat, Papa started the truck engine. He backed the Mazda out, gravel crunching noisily. I waved to my father: a morning ritual of ours. But Papa throttled the engine and sped off to the factory, tires squealing, the truck disappearing into a thin veil of dust.

That almost broke me. I wanted to end the entire thing right then and there. I wanted to go into that chicken house and wring the neck of every goddamn cock sleeping in its coop. But instead I just got on my bike and pedaled off to school.

IX

Later that day, my friend Noon and I decided to stop for an iced coffee in town. I didn't want to be with Noon, but I didn't want to go home, either. I didn't want to be there when Miss Mayuree came to collect the bras. I despised Miss Mayuree—her gold-capped teeth glinting in that beak of a maw, her painted face, her sour gardenia perfume. But above all I hated seeing Mama bow and stoop before her—hated that submissiveness, that feigned gratitude for a paycheck. It made me wonder about our dignity. So when Noon eased up beside me on her bike after school and said, "Hey, stranger, haven't seen you in a while," I just shrugged and said, "'Hey, stranger' yourself."

We'd known each other since we were girls. Noon was the lottery vendor's daughter. Her older sister, Charunee, had notoriously gone to Bangkok and come home calling herself

Charlie, like she hadn't only changed into a man, she'd also become a farang. When we were younger, before her sister decided to become a man, I'd often take Noon home on hot days and we'd scream and prance around the yard while Papa let the chickens loose and Mama pelted us with long jets of water from the hose. We no longer had that kind of friendship, however. Shortly after her sister returned from Bangkok, we both began to go through our own metamorphoses—Noon becoming a lithe, beautiful creature while I grew plump and ordinary in comparison. She gave the boys instant hard-ons; I ignored them altogether. She began to seem vapid and whorish with her relentlessly dollish ways. It was as if, with her sister going to the other side, she'd decided she needed to be twice the woman the rest of us were. For my part, I must have seemed tragic to Noon, with my pale, moonlike face and crispy, uninteresting hair; my indifference to beauty; my thick ankles; my bookishness.

We took our iced coffees to a park bench. That's when we saw Little Jui and Ramon, the Filipino boy, sitting on the sidewalk in front of Old Man Sorachai's teashop. A group of men stood around them in an attentive semicircle. Little Jui gestured dramatically with his hands, occasionally patting the Filipino boy on the back. From what I could tell, Little Jui was narrating his triumphs from the night before; the men responded intermittently with peals of laughter. The Filipino boy stared coolly ahead, tapping his feet arrhythmically against the sidewalk. He smiled every so often, his teeth straight and white and shining in the sun. It seemed impossible that this lanky foreign boy with perfect teeth could humiliate my father. But there he was—the new champion, the boy who'd made my father curse and my mother scream, the boy who'd slaughtered nine of Papa's chickens, the boy who'd won Little Jui's money back. I turned away quickly when he caught me staring at him, but not before—to my chagrin—he beamed a toothy smile in my direction.

"Oh my God don't look," Noon whispered, bending her head toward me. I could detect the scent of jasmine perfume on the nape of her skinny neck. "That Filipino boy is staring at you."

"It's not me he's staring at," I said, laughing. "It's not me he's checking out."

"He is!" Noon insisted, giggling, sipping her coffee. "He's staring at you."

"When did you get this way?" I said. "Don't you think about anything besides penis?"

"Don't be such a killjoy," Noon replied curtly. She looked at the boys flailing around on the new basketball courts Big Jui had recently built for the town. For every superficial civic deed Big Jui did—a basketball court, new bulbs for the town's streetlights, sidewalks repaved, mailboxes on every third scorner—the townspeople agreed to endure his less philan-thropic activities. Mama said it was like being massaged with one hand while getting punched with the other.

"He was, you know," Noon continued, smiling idiotically again. "That boy was staring at you. Swear on my grandmama's grave."

"Okay. Shut up about it. And leave your grandmama out of this."

"He's kind of handsome, actually. He's cute, Ladda." Noon licked her lips, smiled in Ramon's direction. "Nice muscles. Good teeth. Sexy lips."

"He's yours then," I said, slurping the last of my coffee noisily, tossing it into the garbage can beside us. "Doesn't surprise me that you haven't heard, Noon. You're so oblivious. You're so fucking stupid. That boy caused my family a lot of misery."

"What did I ever do to you?" Noon asked, shaking her head. "When did you start hating me? We used to be friends, remember? Of course I heard about your papa; everybody's talking about it. I'm not an idiot, you know. I just thought we were having a bit of fun."

"Sorry," I said quietly, and I really meant it, for I knew I had been unnecessarily cruel. But the look on Noon's face told me that all the apologies in the world wouldn't fix a thing now. "I didn't mean anything by it, Noon," I continued nonetheless. "I'm just having a bad day. You should've been at my house this morning."

"Sure," Noon said. One of the boys on the basketball court called out her name. Noon waved back.

"See you around," she said suddenly, getting up. "Hey," I called after her. I didn't want to be left alone. I was afraid Little Jui would see me, confront me again, this time with that Filipino boy beside him. "I said I was sorry, Noon. And you're right. He is kind of cute."

Noon kicked her bikestand, turned around to face me. "Maybe we can be friends again someday," she said. "But you have to play nice, Ladda."

"Noon, I said I was—"

"Whatever," she said, getting on her bike. "Later."

I wanted to leap from my seat and tear the ringlets from her scalp. But instead I just watched her bike toward the basketball court, her long hair waving behind her. In front of the teashop, Little Jui was still spinning his yarn for the men; he limped around now in what was an imitation either of Papa's cocks or of Papa himself. The men laughed, which only encouraged Little Jui; he seemed like a toddler pleased by adult approval. I noticed that Ramon had disappeared while Noon and I were talking. I panicked. Because Noon was right—the boy *did* smile at me—and I was afraid that Ramon was approaching me unseen, that he would startle me with a light touch on the shoulder, a whisper in the ear.

I decided to go home. I started biking through the park toward the main road. As I passed the basketball court, I spotted Ramon there, scurrying for a loose ball. The other boys converged upon him while Noon clapped from the sidelines like an idiot. After a brief struggle, Ramon emerged with the ball. He stood there smiling under the sun, his chest glistening with sweat, the ball nestled in the crook of an arm.

He waved at me.

I looked away, put my head down, pedaled as fast as I could through the park. By the time I got to the main road, I couldn't tell if the heat in my chest was from the biking, from the hot sun, or from the way that foreigner had waved while Noon and the other boys looked in my direction.

X

When I got home, Miss Mayuree was still on the porch with Mama. Two of her men loaded the lingerie boxes into her sleek blue sedan. Mama smiled, nodded blankly. I went to the chicken house to find Papa. He was doing the weekly cleaning. I went inside and helped him change the water pans and sanitize the coops.

While we cleaned, Papa told me he had a new strategy. There was no way his cocks could outfight those Filipino purebreds, he said; that was his mistake. The purebreds were too large, too strong for that. In the Philippines, those chickens guard houses, attack thieves in the night. Dogs feared them. There wasn't a Thai chicken that could outfight a Filipino purebred; any self-respecting cockfighter knew that. The only way to beat one, Papa said, was to own one. But we didn't own any Filipino purebreds, I reminded Papa. We owned nothing but mongrel hatchlings bought from local farmers, cocks born to crow at the sun and strut around the yard.

"Fear," he said proudly. "That's the key, Ladda. That's the solution."

I squinted at him.

Papa told me that cocks know no fear. If they felt their territory was at stake, they'd probably fight a truck. He needed to teach the chickens fear. He needed to teach them how to dodge. If he could get his cocks to bob and weave like nimble boxers from the murderous advances of the Filipino purebreds, they might have a chance. Papa skipped around the chicken house as if to demonstrate the idea. I thought he'd lost his mind.

"C'mon," he said, whipping his head, fists swinging at his sides. "Hit me."

"Papa," I said.

"Hit me," he said, smiling playfully. "Give it a try. I'll be one of the cocks. You be one of the Filipino purebreds."

"Papa," I said again, bending down to scoop a pile of droppings with a dustpan, watching them cascade into the garbage bag. But Papa kept hopping around like some crazy. I stared at him with the garbage bag in one hand. Papa started clucking like a chicken then, put fists to armpits and flapped his elbows, bounding wildly around me. I laughed.

"Hit me, hit me, hit me!" he yelled, laughing too. "Give it your best shot, Ladda. Bok-bok! Bok-bok!"

"You're crazy," I said. "Wait till I tell Mama about this."

"C'mon, you Filipino purebred! Give it your best shot!" He reached out with a hand and slapped me jokingly on the side of the head. "Bok-bok! Bok-bok!"

"Papa!"

But Papa just kept on jumping around, reaching out to cuff me again and again. I became exasperated. I suddenly started thinking about the way he'd driven off earlier that day, ignoring my wave, and how he seemed so different now, the same old Papa, like nothing had happened. So I reached out and swung the bag of chicken shit at his face. I trusted Papa to dodge. But the blow hit him squarely on the ear, bursting the bag, chicken shit hailing down all around us.

Papa looked at me stunned. For a second, I was afraid I'd really hurt him. "Nice shot," he said, grinning sheepishly.

"Let's hope the cocks are faster, Papa," I said, relieved by his good humor. "I'm no Filipino purebred, you know. I'm no murderous chicken."

Papa told Mama about the new strategy over dinner. Mama nodded quietly. Miss Mayuree's visits always put Mama in a sour, insular mood. This time, Miss Mayuree had upped the monthly quota to a thousand, though without an increase in pay. Work was scarce; Mama had agreed to the new quota.

"I've had enough," Mama said, ignoring Papa. "I've had enough of that miserly, harlot widow and her goddamn lingerie."

"Did you hear what I just said?" Papa asked. "About the chickens?"

"Sure," Mama replied. "You're teaching your chickens fear."

"It's genius," Papa declared.

"Sure," Mama said again. "You're a genius. But I really don't care if you teach your chickens how to flush a toilet. Because you know what would truly be genius, Wichian? What would truly be genius is if you get us back the eleven thousand on Sunday. This ship is sinking fast."

XI

I saw Little Jui again the next afternoon. The Range Rover was parked outside the high school. Before I could get to my bike, Dam and Dang stopped me by the barbed-wire fence. "Miss," Dam said, tapping my shoulder, while his partner stared down at me, gut heaving like some gigantic melon pulsing beneath his shirt. "Come with us."

"I don't think so," I said. I tried to walk past them, but Dang nudged me back with a quick hand. "Get your hands off me!" I cried. Some of the students looked in our direction but—seeing Dam and Dang—decided to ignore the scene, resume their after-school chattering.

"No need to make a fuss, miss," Dam said, raising his pudgy hands as if taking an oath of innocence, and I remembered then that these two were responsible for the bruises on Papa's face, bruises which were only beginning to heal. "The boss just wants to talk to you," Dang said. I saw the Range Rover across the street, Little Jui smiling out the back window. Ramon, the Filipino boy, was sitting next to him, staring at me over Little Jui's shoulder.

"Just come with us, miss," Dam said again. "We don't mean any harm."

"You assholes," I said, gritting my teeth. Then, to my own surprise, I spat at them both—one, then the other—thin strings of spittle landing on their shirtfronts. "That's for what you did to my father."

"Now, there's no need for that," Dam whispered, grabbing me briskly by the forearm, and my heart leapt, more from the gesture's brutishness than from the pain it inflicted. I tried to pull away. I heard Noon then, recognized her bright, chirpy laughter. I tried to make eye contact, but Noon seemed oblivious, deep in some mating dance: smiling, hands fluttering, body leaning into a boy's smile.

"If you want to be treated like a lady," Dam hissed, tightening his grip, "start acting like one."

"Okay," I said. "Sure." So I bent down and bit his thick, hairy fingers, his skin taut and salty between my teeth, his thick bones creaking like a plum pit in my jaw. Dam winced and yapped, tried to yank his fingers away. I wished Papa could see me. I wanted to break the skin, feel the warm gush of blood

on my tongue, but Dam managed to pull himself free by yanking at my hair with his other hand. His partner Dang grabbed
me by the waist, hoisted me up, and carried me toward the
Range Rover. I kicked and screamed, his ropy arms like a noose
tightening around my abdomen, Little Jui's smiling face moving closer and closer with every step.

"Hey! Put her down!" a voice called out from behind us.

To my surprise, Dang set me down in the street. Little
Jui laughed from the backseat of the Range Rover. Ramon eyed
me silently, his mouth a straight thin line. When I turned
around, I saw Noon lunging at Dang, pelting his chest with a
flurry of impotent slaps. He tried to grab her flailing arms, told
her to cut the nonsense. All the other students stopped and
looked in our direction now.

The security guard ran toward us from his box outside
the high school gate, a hand on his baton. "Is there a problem here?" he asked, looking at Dang, who now had both of
Noon's wrists in his hands. The guard said those words sheepishly, like he'd heard them somewhere else, on television
perhaps. He was a young, sickly boy known more for his way
with the high school girls than his ability to fend off whatever dangers necessitated his presence. He was just another
one of the town's many pretenses, especially where the law
was concerned.

"Yes, there is," Noon said impatiently, struggling against
Dang's grip. He let her go. Dam stalked up behind me, nurs-
ing his hand. I heard him call me a cunt.

"No problem, guy," Little Jui said from the backseat of the Range Rover. "No problem at all." Little Jui reached out and waved a red hundred-baht note in the security guard's face. "We were just having some fun, guy. Just horsing around."

The security guard kept looking back and forth helplessly between the note fanning before him, Little Jui's smile, and me. "Just a bit of fun, guy," Little Jui said again. He tossed the note at the security guard, the bill flopping in the air before landing at his feet. And all that time I felt Ramon staring at me over Little Jui's shoulder.

"You can go back to your little box now," Little Jui said. The security guard looked at me. He bent down and picked up the note from the ground. "Take it elsewhere," he said to Little Jui, tucking the money into his breast pocket. "Go have fun somewhere else."

"Hey," I said as the security guard walked away. The students started chattering again. "These people are trying to kidnap me!"

"C'mon, Ladda," Noon said, reaching for my arm. "Let's get out of here."

When I looked back, Dang had already started the Range Rover while Dam settled himself into the passenger seat, his face still red with pain. Little Jui leaned out the window and pinched my cheek.

"I'm gonna get you next time," he said, sucking obscenely at his lips, fingering my chin. "I'm gonna get you good." Ramon looked at me, brow furrowed in consternation.

"*You have no idea about the people you're working for, do you,*" I wanted to say to him. I reached out and tried to grab Little Jui's fingers, thinking I might bite again; but Dang had already pulled the car away, Little Jui's laughter fading down the road.

"You okay?" Noon asked as the car disappeared. "Fine," I said, rubbing my forearm, blood like lava in my veins. "Thanks."

We picked up our bicycles and walked away from the high school. The bike chains ticked between us as the sun elongated our shadows. I wanted to hug Noon then; I wanted to apologize for being cruel the day before. She had surprised me with her bravery. I wanted to tell Noon how afraid I'd been when that goon picked me up and carried me across the street. How suffocated. How helpless. How—for the first time in my life—truly endangered.

Before we parted ways, I asked Noon if she'd ever heard about Papa's sister.

"Yeah," she said nonchalantly. "The Slobbering Slut. That's what the men in the teashops used to call her."

"My God," I said. "How come you never told me about it?"

"I guess it's one of those things," Noon said, shrugging.

"I need to get out of this town," I said.

Noon nodded. "Call me when you figure out how, okay? I'm bored to death with these country boys. Speaking of which, what does Little Jui want from you anyway?"

"I don't know," I said. "But I swear I'm gonna move his asshole to where his face is." Noon laughed. "Make sure I'm there when you do that," she said. She got on her bike, tucked the back of her dress beneath her. "See you around," she said. "Say hi to your papa for me. Tell him I'll be praying for his chickens this Sunday."

XII

Teaching chickens fear takes time, and Papa didn't have enough of it that week. So he went that Sunday with only one cock—a weak, colicky creature quarantined out back because it had been plucking its own feathers. The chicken was diseased. Papa knew he would lose, but he needed to send Little Jui a message. Regularity was the message, he said. He wasn't affected by last week's losses was the message. But Mama said, "Here's a better message, Wichian. Don't show up. Find a new hobby. Collect stamps. Raise carp. Exercise. Help me with the lingerie. Do something civilized for once." But Papa just laughed it off.

He came back that Sunday afternoon carrying the diseased chicken in a bloody plastic bag. Mama looked into the bag and said that if Papa wanted the thing slaughtered, he should've asked her to do it—at least then she'd be able to distinguish breasts from thighs from wings from feet from intestines. At least we'd have a useful chicken, Mama said. Now all we have is a mess. And when Papa told her over dinner that he'd lost another thousand, Mama said, "Enough is enough, Wichian. Let them win. Little Jui's not out to kill you any-more. He's decided to take all your money."

But Papa shrugged and said the loss was expected. Los-ing had been part of his strategy. The diseased cock was going to die anyway. Once he taught his chickens how to be afraid, he'd start winning his money back. He'd humiliate Little Jui and that Filipino boy. He'd be champion again.

Still, he told us that something unexpected happened at the pit that afternoon: The men had cheered Little Jui, ap-plauded the Filipino boy and his purebreds.

"It's like they have no memory," Papa said. "It's like they forgot what he did to me. They treated him like a veteran. And they treated me like I was some amateur."

"People like winners," Mama said.

"How can they forget what his family's done?"

"People like winners," Mama said again.

"I heard you the first time, Saiya."

"Give it up," Mama said, collecting our plates. "It's a lost cause. That boy's making a fool of you *and* he's taking all our money. It's probably his father's idea, that's what I think. Big Jui arranged to have that Filipino boy sent over, didn't he? He's probably laughing at you now, Wichian."

I looked at Papa. I thought I saw his face darken, a light shadow pass over his features, and I wondered if this had always happened, if—in my ignorance—I'd always missed the severity of Papa's features whenever he was confronted with Big Jui's name.

"That man," Papa said, "has nothing to do with this, Saiya. It's between me and the boy."

"Sure," Mama said. "Whatever you say, Wichian."

"Besides," Papa said, "I'm going to win next week. You just watch. Once I'm through training the cocks, they'll mince those Filipino purebreds."

"Well, good luck to you, Wichian," Mama said, shaking her head. "Have fun trying. But before you teach your chickens how to dodge a speeding bullet, let me remind you that you've lost twelve thousand now. In case you haven't heard, nobody's betting against that Filipino boy."

"You just watch," Papa said grimly to Mama. "Have a little faith in my chickens."

XIII

We rarely saw Papa that week. He'd come home from the factory and retire immediately to the chicken house. I'd occasionally watch Papa go through his routine: massaging the cocks' thighs, bathing them, purifying the feed, sharpening the spurs, making sure they received the proper amount of sun. If Papa was teaching the chickens fear, I couldn't see how. They were getting the usual treatment, the kind of impeccable care that—according to Mama—would end a lot of suffering if the town's women and children were treated the same.

Sunday drew near. I didn't see Little Jui; again, I had begun to dread the outside world after our last encounter. Open air made me nervous. In my mind, the Range Rover loomed around every corner. Noon invited me out several times, but I told her I needed to help Mama with the lingerie. I rushed headlong between home and school, taking the long way along the small path reserved for dirt bikes and water buffaloes that ran through the rubber grove. Better the strays, I thought, than Little Jui and his goons. I considered telling Mama about Little Jui's advances, but she had become unflappably morose—complaining at all times about Papa, about the chickens, about Miss Mayuree—and I didn't want to aggravate her mood. Besides, I didn't know if Little Jui's menace would have real consequences or if it was simply designed to frighten me and, as a result, Papa as well. Many hours were spent considering the possibilities, none innocent, while Papa tended to his chickens outside my bedroom window. I started having strange, barbaric dreams.

Friday morning, after he'd run the cocks, Papa was out in the yard with what looked like a black kitchen radio in his hands. Two chickens flapped around the yard before him, sparring without their spurs, lurching at one another, their bodies clashing in the air as a bright bursting of color. I went to help Mama with breakfast. She turned to me and said, "The insanity, Ladda. Just look at him."

I looked. I realized then that the kitchen radio Papa held in his hands was actually the radio for a remote-control car. I realized, too, that there weren't two cocks in the yard at all—there was only one. The other was a rubber chicken attached to the roof of the remote-control car. Papa'd painted plumage on the decoy's synthetic body, splotches of green and ochre and yellow and white. It was a childish paint job: on closer look, the decoy looked more like a clown than a gamecock. Nonetheless, Papa tried to chase the cock with the contraption. Unfazed, the cock kept launching at his rubber compatriot, toppling it over, Papa cursing each time before righting the car once more, only to have the chicken knock the contraption down again, the car's wheels whizzing wildly in the air, jerking the fake chicken with its momentum so that it wiggled with artificial life. On and on it went, and with each blow the cock landed on his rubber opponent, he seemed to gather courage rather than fear, though that courage soon turned to irritation: The cock didn't even bother to leap into the air to deliver his blows anymore, he just charged absent-mindedly before turning his attention elsewhere as Papa prepared the contraption again. The cock knew as Papa knew as Mama and I knew that a rubber chicken attached to a remote-control car was nothing to be afraid of. I realized then the extent of my father's desperation. Papa, I understood now, didn't know what he was doing.

"Wow," I said to Mama. "That's interesting."

"I've seen it all," Mama muttered, shaking her head. Papa tried a few more times. The cock rushed doggedly at the contraption, pecked curiously at the overturned toy car.

Then Papa dashed the controls to the ground and smashed them with a few violent stomps. The box shattered into tiny black pieces, springs and coils and wires and plastic parts scattering across the yard. Thinking it might be feed, the cock waddled over and inspected the pieces strewn around Papa's feet.

"Oh God," Mama said. "Go calm him down, Ladda. He's not coming to breakfast like that."

Before I could step off the porch, however, Papa's anger had moved on from the remote control to the cock itself. He kicked it. The cock leapt into the air. Papa lunged at the creature with his hands; I thought he would wring its neck right then and there. But the cock leapt defiantly back into Papa's face. Papa fell, surprised by the cock's retaliation, and the cock jumped feetfirst into my father's face again, tried to sink its sharpened talons into Papa's cheeks, mad clucks like tiny screams echoing in the morning. Papa tried to shove the cock off his face, batted it with his hands, but the cock kept leaping toward him, a relentless flurry of feathers.

I cried out for Papa, ran toward him, but he didn't hear me. After a short struggle, he managed to grab the cock by the neck and bash its body against the ground. I thought Papa would sever the cock's head from its body with his bashing, but then he gathered the creature into his arms and held it to his chest with its beak facing forward, its wings trapped between his knees—the safest position (I'd been told for as long as I could remember) to handle a gamecock. The chicken thrashed violently for a moment before settling down, its chest heaving in Papa's grip, its head skittering to and fro.

"Stupid," I heard Papa mumble when I approached. I didn't know if he was talking to the chicken or to himself. "Papa," I said. "Are you okay?" He turned to me suddenly, eyes wide as if in a trance. He'd never looked at me like that before. I was afraid Papa would turn his rage on me now. I stepped back. He wasn't Papa anymore; he'd become somebody else. He looked crazed. The cock had left a few light gashes on his face. Blood rose to the skin's surface like war paint. With that chicken fussing between his knees, Papa looked like one of the wildmen in a documentary about the Amazon I'd seen years ago, when we bought our first color set from his winnings. But then Papa came back to himself. The madness left his eyes. He smiled at me sheepishly.

"Here," he said, holding out the creature with both hands. "Take the chicken," he said, as if he'd been waiting all morning for me to do the task. I gathered the creature into my arms, trapped its body between my knees. The cock began to purr, its body vibrating delicately against my thighs. I thought I could feel its tiny chicken heart fluttering beneath the skin. On the other side of the yard, the remote-control car lay on its side like a toy some fickle child had abandoned. Papa wiped his face with his shirt, light streaks of blood dotting the fabric. The gashes were superficial. He squatted before me.

"What am I going to do with you?" Papa said grimly. I thought he was speaking to me; I didn't know what to say. But then I realized that Papa was speaking to the chicken. The cock nudged my father lightly on the nose as if to apologize. Papa held the chicken by its neck to still its frenetic head. "Why won't you cooperate?"

"Are you okay?" I asked again. My heart was still hopping wildly in its cage from the way Papa had looked at me, crouched on the ground with those gashes on his face, that chicken between his knees, those eyes strange in their sockets. The chicken struggled, wriggled its wings between my thighs. Papa took it back into his arms. "Go back inside, Ladda," he said. "I won't be having breakfast this morning."

"No," I said. I don't know why I refused—it seemed somebody else had spoken the word even as it rolled off my tongue—but I'd been filled with anger toward my father at that moment. I would've defied him even if he'd tried to embrace me. "No, Papa. Come inside. Give it a rest."

Papa smiled sheepishly again. Then he just stood there looking at me with his mouth half-opened. I wanted to ask Papa about his sister then. Ever since talking to Noon, I wanted to know my aunt as somebody other than the Slobbering Slut. I wanted to know her by another name. Because, by then, the moniker had become the substance of my nightmares: spittle and blood and sex and men grunting in back alleys and a lunatic's laughter answering their cries. I thought things might be tolerable if I could know her name. I said, "Papa—your sister—," but Papa looked at me strangely, eyebrows raised, like I wasn't making any sense.

"Sister?" he asked. "What are you talking about, Ladda?"

"Mama told me," I said. "Mama told me the other day."

"That's ridiculous," Papa said.

"But Mama said your sister and Big Jui—"

"Ladda," Papa interrupted. "You should know better. People make up all sorts of nonsense about each other to pass the time."

He smiled at me then, but this time Papa's smile seemed writ with cunning: too many teeth, too much lifting of the lips, too much feigned delight in his eyes. I thought, for a second, of the smile that hung from Little Jui's face in the Range Rover. Papa was lying. Papa was denying his own sister.

So I left him there with his chicken in the yard.

XIV

Papa lost. And then he lost again. And then, the week after, he lost once more. There were only five chickens left in the chicken house; we were poorer by the thousands now. Mama stopped talking to him altogether, which didn't really matter because Papa had sunk into himself more and more with each Sunday loss.

I no longer sought my father's company. After he'd lied about his own sister, I felt as if I were seeing him for the first time in my life, stripped of any daughterly admiration. I wasn't angry with him; I was frightened. I wondered if Papa would deny me, too, if Little Jui had his way with me. I spent days in my room, burrowed deep in my books. The house became silent; we'd become mimes acting out the play of our lives.

One morning, a Thursday, Mama threatened to leave. She didn't marry a lowlife gambler, she said. If he went back to the pit, he would be coming home to an empty house. She said Miss Mayuree had offered a room in her house. Though Mama had made many similar threats through the years, she'd never brought somebody outside our family into the fray. I didn't know whether she'd really called Miss Mayuree or whether Mama thought that her name might convey to Papa the severity of her threat. When I asked her about it over sewing one evening, she simply shrugged and said, "We'll see."

Papa's tactics became more desperate. He'd scrapped the remote-control car and, instead, started sparring with the chickens himself every morning. He'd put on thick construction gloves and charge at them. All he got for his efforts were a few more scars. The chickens became wary of him, though they seemed far from afraid. Whenever he entered the chicken house, their angry clucks would echo through the property and I'd wonder if chickens were smart enough to start a mutiny.

A passel of strays broke into the chicken house that Friday night. I woke to their barking, to my father's cursing and kicking at them, to the chickens' frightened chattering. When I looked out the window, I saw a stray with a chicken between its teeth, trotting away with his head held high while the others lingered around him, waiting to share the bounty. Papa stood at the chicken-house door holding a broom. When the strays disappeared, he sat on the ground, dropped the broom, and buried his face in his hands. I thought he was crying, but soon I saw that he was merely massaging his temples. He disappeared into the chicken house again. I wished then that the strays had taken all of Papa's chickens. I watched the rubber trees, hoping they would return again. But they didn't. I only heard their yaps and howls out there, fighting over the chicken.

Little Jui called the house the next afternoon.

"Hey, sexy," he panted. "Haven't seen you around."

I hung up. But he called right back. I just stood there staring at the phone, thinking I might smash it to pieces.

"Who's that?" Mama asked as the phone's ringing echoed through our house. She must've known from the way I looked at her, because she pushed me aside and picked up the receiver.

"Listen to me, you little fuck," she said into the phone. "Leave us alone. Call again, and I'll slit your throat from ear to ear." I thought she would hang up then, but Mama just stood there listening to Little Jui, the anger slowly dissipating from her face. After a few minutes, she gently hung up the receiver.

"What did he say? What did that asshole want?"

Mama looked at me seriously; I thought she would reprimand me for swearing. "His money," Mama said finally. "Your father owes a lot more than we think." I asked Mama how much. "Too much," Mama said, shaking her head. "He's coming to take the Mazda. He said he's coming to take it if your father doesn't give him his money."

"No."

"Go tell him," she said, nodding in the direction of the chicken house.

When I walked into the chicken house, I saw that the strays had made a considerable mess of things the night before. Feathers everywhere. Overturned water pans. Feed spilled from broken bags. Splotches of dried chicken blood on one of the straw beds. Papa was slicking a cock's feathers—wiping its body down with a wet sponge—his back turned to me.

"He's coming to take the Mazda," I said to his back. Papa didn't turn around. He just nodded at the chicken. "Did you hear me, Papa? He's coming to take the truck." Papa paused, then reached into his pockets. He threw me the keys to the Mazda. Then he turned his attention back to the chicken. The chicken cooed at the moisture. I wanted to grab Papa by the shoulders and shake him then.

"How could you let this happen?" I asked him. "How much did you actually lose?"

But Papa wouldn't answer. I waited, watching him wipe down that chicken. I noticed a strange kinship between them.

The chicken suddenly looked like some evolutionary relative of my father's. Its long, spindly neck seemed to duplicate Papa's erect carriage; its spiky verdigris crown feathers were not unlike Papa's gray, unruly hair. What's more, there seemed something eerie about the way my father's gaunt, emaciated features seemed mirrored in the creature's stony profile. Beady eyes. Sunken cheeks. Aquiline beak. Even the chicken's barklike talons had their counterpart, in Papa's slender fingers and jagged nails.

I thought Papa had said something to me. But then I realized he was whispering to the chicken.

I left, the keys to the Mazda hot in my hands. I thought of getting in the Mazda and driving off. But I didn't know where I would go. Perhaps I would pick up Noon from her house. Perhaps she would know.

"What did he say?" Mama asked. I put the keys on the kitchen counter, walked to my room. "Ladda," Mama called after me. "What did he say?"

I sat down and tried to study for a trigonometry exam. But I couldn't concentrate. Right angles, hypotenuses, tangents, sine, cosine: They all passed before my eyes without meaning. After a while, those lines and equations seemed like just another sport men had created to pass their time on this earth, and it occurred to me then that the difference between cockfighting and trigonometry was a difference in degree, not a difference in kind. Both were diversions designed to amuse, games with varying odds for victory. All human activity suddenly seemed to me composed of such sport: We each chose the game we thought would yield the most for us and our own. We gambled, gambled selfishly, gambled more than we could afford, the odds staggeringly stacked in somebody else's favor. Papa, of course, was an obvious example. But Mama, too. She'd spent a good part of her life making bras for anonymous women living in faraway places she'd probably never see. She called it an honest living. But, as I sat in that room, those triangles staring at me from the textbook, it didn't seem like much of a living. Mama'd wagered her strength and her labor and the sweat off her brow and the high-noon decades of her life, but in the end she only stood to make Miss Mayuree wealthy. Noon, too, with her monomania for boys, the way she indiscriminately anted her affections in the hopes of unattainable rewards. Because love was the biggest gamble of them all. Love had the worst odds. The rules were convoluted and mystifying and changing all the time. Even Papa's sister must've known this. The house would always win that bastard game, so I decided at that moment to become its undying enemy forever.

I put the book away. When I looked up, I saw the Range Rover parked in our driveway, Little Jui and his goons and that Filipino boy Ramon getting out of the car. I moved to the side of the window so they would not see me.

Mama went out, a fist around the Mazda's keys. Little Jui had a bouquet of roses nestled in his arms. As Little Jui spoke, Mama kept shaking her head, like she couldn't believe what he was telling her. She kept looking toward the chicken house, waiting for Papa to appear. But he never did. After some more talking, Little Jui handed Mama the roses and Mama gave him the keys to the Mazda, as if making an equal barter. Little Jui tossed the keys to Dam and the goons went to Papa's truck. Little Jui got back in the Range Rover with Ramon and soon they all disappeared down the road. Mama just stood there with an astonished look on her face, as if the Mazda had come to life and decided on its own to accompany the Range Rover into town.

She came into my room.

"These are for you," she said, throwing the bouquet onto my bed, a few loose petals flying across my sheets. "I don't want them, Mama," I said curtly.

"That's it, Ladda," she yelled suddenly. "I've had enough. Pack your bags." Mama's hands shook involuntarily. She stared at them, clasped them tightly together to stop the shaking. "Mama," I said. But before I could ask her to calm down, she sat on my bed and seemed to slump from some enormous, invisible weight. She started to cry, hands in her lap, lips quivering, eyes staring angrily ahead. I went over, sat down beside her, put an arm around her shoulders.

"C'mon, Mama."

She wiped snot with the back of a hand. She steeled herself against more tears. "I'll kill him before he can go back to that cockpit."

"Mama—"

"What's with the roses, Ladda?" Mama asked. "He said you two were in love. I told him I'd cut off his dick before he ever got near you again.

"He's been bothering me, Mama," I said, relieved to be telling her at last. "I ignore him, though," I said. "I hate him more than you can imagine. I'd cut his dick off too, Mama."

Mama patted my knee. She got up and gathered the roses into her arms. She walked over to my window and opened the screen. "Hey," she yelled, throwing the roses out the window toward the chicken house. They landed impotently a few feet away. "I hope you're satisfied," Mama said. "Have fun walking to work from now on."

XV

Saturday night, Papa came into the house and said this would be the last time. He asked us for patience. We stared at him blankly. He was going to bring all the remaining cocks to the cockpit tomorrow, he informed us, staring at his feet as if embarrassed. Win or lose, he wouldn't be going back again. He was sorry. He never meant to hurt anybody. He looked at Mama, looked at me, waited for an answer. But Mama just said the house would be empty when he returned. Papa nodded, like a criminal accepting his sentence, and walked out of the house, dragging his slippers across the yard, his head hanging limply from his neck.

Mama got up and called Miss Mayuree. As she talked into the phone, I abandoned my dinner and walked outside. Years before, my feet would've led me to the chicken house, to Papa; they wanted to go there now. The air was thick with humidity. The monsoons were coming in a few months. The mosquitoes were hatching. The first of the season's cicadas had arrived to creak and whir in the rubber trees. I listened to them. My feet began to lead me toward their sound. I walked across the yard, I don't know why. I suppose I simply wanted to get away.

When I arrived at the ditch, I hopped over it easily, and soon I found myself under the dark rubber canopy, all around me the shrill soprano cries of the cicadas in the eaves, their song reverberating through the trees like prayer echoing around some temple pavilion. The air thrummed with the noise. When I was a child, I'd always been afraid of the rubber grove, with its strays howling like so many ghosts during the nighttime hours. But now, standing in that pitch-black forest, watching Mama's light in the kitchen window and Papa's light in the chicken house shining through the thicket like two equidistant flames, I felt safe among the trees and I felt that out there, outside the grove, was where real danger lay. There were no ghouls here—just animals foraging for food, mating and fighting and singing their songs.

I sat down cross-legged. I felt I might be able to sit there forever. But then the feeling passed. *That's your life,* the cicadas seemed to say to me as I looked out at our property. *That small patch of ground. Those are the people you love. Those two distant lights. That's your papa in the chicken house. That's your mama in the kitchen. You can't hide in here forever.* I got up and walked farther into the trees, turning my back upon the property, thinking I might get myself lost. But the cicadas told me no. They reminded me that this wasn't even a real rubber forest, just an abandoned plantation. I'd only end up in town if I went any farther. So, after a while, I turned around and walked back toward the house. I paused at the ditch, thinking I might go into the trees again, thinking I might never come back, wondering how long it would take for Mama and Papa to notice my absence. But that feeling soon passed as well. I went back over the ditch.

XVI

Sunday, under a bright and cloudless sky, Mama and I watched Papa from the porch as he put the four remaining cocks into a rusted wheelbarrow. Mama stood there chewing her cuticles, leaning against the house. In a quiet voice Papa said he'd understand if we weren't here when he got back. He said he loved us both. He said he would put in overtime at the roofing factory. He said, "I'm sorry, Saiya," but Mama looked right through him. He stood there dumbly, lips parted as if he might say something else, and then he walked out the driveway, his whole body leaning into the wheelbarrow's weight while the chickens clucked noisily.

"Oi," Mama muttered, still staring at the empty road. "I guess we should pack our bags."

"You sure, Mama?"

"Of course I'm sure," Mama said sternly. "I'll call Miss Mayuree now."

"I don't know, Mama—"

"What don't you know, Ladda?" Mama scoffed. "What are you so unsure about? You want to stay? Fine. Stay. Suit yourself."

Mama went inside the house. For a while, I sat on the porch and stared at the wheelbarrow's tracks on the driveway, its light lines trailing through the gravel like veins. There was a cold, eerie silence in the yard—this was the first time, I realized, that our property didn't echo with the noises of chickens. I heard Mama pick up the phone to call Miss Mayuree. "Yes," I heard her say. "Thank you, ma'am. You're too kind. Yes. Just a few days. Of course we will. Thank you so much."

Mama came back, stood in the doorway with a hand on her hip. She said Miss Mayuree was sending somebody to pick us up. I turned to face her. "Are we really leaving, Mama? Is this it? You don't ever want to see him again?" Mama didn't answer me at first. She just crouched down and packed her sewing machine into its plastic case. "We'll see, " she said. "It's not up to me. It's up to your father." I stood. "Don't you love him, Mama?" She smiled. "Of course I do," she said. "But that's not the point, Ladda. Love or no love, the men in this world don't leave women with much choice sometimes. It's all we can do to hang on to our dignity."

I nodded as if I understood, though what she'd said made no sense whatsoever. What did a woman's dignity have to do with anything? I wanted to ask her. What kind of dignity would we have by going to Miss Mayuree? Wasn't it Papa's dignity in the balance? Wouldn't we just add to the sum total of his humiliation by leaving him? I felt a slow, recalcitrant heat blooming in my temples. After a moment, the heat seemed like some dogged flower pushing against the top of my skull. Mama must've sensed my distress; she walked over and reached out to touch one of my shoulders.

"C'mon, Ladda," Mama said softly. "Go get your things. It's not the end of the world. We'll probably be back by the end of the week." I shrugged her hand off my shoulder. "This isn't permanent," she added. "At least I don't think it is. I just want to scare some sense into him. We can't go on like this anymore."

I walked to my room. I sat on my bed, watched the shadows list back and forth across the floor. The throbbing in my head had traveled to the rest of my body; I felt as if I might combust, burst into flames, liquefy from the inside out. I grabbed the wooden hairbrush on the nightstand and flung it across the room. The brush bounced off the wall, landed quietly on its bristles. It was a disappointing gesture. I caught my reflection in the mirror and felt terribly foolish. I got up and started to pack my things.

Soon, Miss Mayuree's blue sedan appeared. The driver honked, got out of the car, and opened the trunk. He didn't say anything, though every so often he would smile knowingly at me. After a few trips, we managed to pack all our bags. We got in the backseat, the vinyl sticky against our skin. Upcountry music played softly on the radio. As we gathered speed along the road, Mama kept staring at her feet, as if she couldn't bear to watch the house disappear behind us.

Miss Mayuree was waiting. She smiled as we pulled into her driveway. She put an arm around my shoulder. "You poor thing," she said, shaking her head. "You poor, poor thing." She smelled like baby powder. She wore a belt with a large gold buckle that glinted when she breathed. A fat, smiling Buddha had been carved into the buckle, and I stared at the thing, afraid that if I met Miss Mayuree's eyes I might say something rude.

She showed us the back room where we would be sleeping, a small concrete cavern behind the kitchen. A solitary lightbulb hung by a wire from the ceiling. Mold hugged the cracks along the bare gray walls. On one wall, there was a calendar from the lingerie company, a picture of a skinny white woman with eyes closed, slender hands cupping gigantic breasts. "This is where the maids used to sleep before I built them their quarters," Miss Mayuree said proudly. Mama thanked her while I stared at the moth-eaten pallet in the center of the room. "Just help around the house when you can, Saiya," Miss Mayuree said. Mama nodded demurely and thanked her once again.

"Ladda," Mama said after Miss Mayuree left us. "Manners. She's doing us a favor."

"I don't care if she wipes my ass, Mama," I said. "She gives me the creeps."

"Now, now," she said. "Now, now."

We didn't say much to each other the rest of the day. After unpacking, we went to the yard to help trim the hedges. We introduced ourselves to the maids, picked up shears and gloves. As we worked, Mama told them our predicament and they nodded absentmindedly, as if they'd heard the story before. Every so often, a pickup truck would drive by and people would peer out their windows to look at Mama and me working in Miss Mayuree's yard. The rumormongers would have themselves a party today, gabbing about our family.

Miss Mayuree came out and told me she didn't want me doing any work. She said I should rest. "You poor thing," she said again. "You've been through so much." She thought she was being kind; it made me want to trim her hedges even more. I snipped my shears enthusiastically, pretended that the branches were the blue-green veins on Miss Mayuree's pale, wrinkled neck. "She's just like her mother," she said to Mama. "A good worker."

We worked on the hedges well into the evening. I kept expecting to see Papa pushing his wheelbarrow down the road. I wondered how he was doing at the cockpit today. I wondered if he'd already come home to find the house empty.

As Mama and I lay down side-by-side on the foam pallet that night, I realized I hadn't slept with my mother in a long time. I realized, too, that this was the first time I had slept in a room that was not my own. When I turned in that darkness to face the far wall, I half expected to find a window letting in light from Papa's chicken house; instead, I found the woman cupping her breasts on the lingerie calendar. I listened to Mama's breathing; I could tell from its short, choppy rhythm that she was still awake. I closed my eyes.

I had a dream. I dreamed that Papa and Mama were running a sideshow involving chickens. The show took place in our front yard. People came from all over to watch. Even the strays had stationed themselves on the road in front of our house, howling happily along with the crowd. I watched everything from above. The town and the streets and the rubber trees and our property lay before me like a model train set. All of Papa's chickens were there, alive. Papa made them fly through hoops of fire while Mama stood beside him smiling and gesturing in a glittering pink and lavender bikini. Then Mama stood against a makeshift wall as Papa threw the chickens at her like knives, the chickens gliding gracefully through the air, their sharpened beaks missing Mama's face and body by inches, the crowd oohing and aahing in anxious delight with each throw. The trick completed, Mama put the chickens into her mouth, slowly swallowing each one whole, their bodies and their feet wriggling between her lips before disappearing into her cavity. The crowd gasped in horror. Papa produced a top hat and pulled out the chickens one by one and everybody, even I standing above it all, laughed and clapped and cheered him loudly. As I did so, I realized that everybody was looking up at me, that all those tiny little people were pointing at me, standing above them in their sky like a god. Somebody screamed. The crowd began to scatter like flies, even Mama and Papa and the chickens. I called out to them, told them in a booming voice to come back. A trembling rage passed through my body. I wanted to reach out and squash them all between my fingers, but as I began to pick one out from that model world below me, I felt a hand touch my shoulder, and I woke up to find Mama peering at me through the darkness.

"Ladda." She was whispering into my face. "C'mon, baby. Wake up. We have to go. Your father's in the hospital."

XVII

Noon had come to Miss Mayuree's house that night, pounding on the back door, asking for my mother and me. Mama was still awake when she heard the pounding. She bolted to the door. A few minutes later, the three of us were walking the three kilometers to the hospital in town. Noon didn't know what had happened. She'd only heard her father say, when he got home from the cockpit, that Papa'd been hurt and was now in the hospital. "It's a shame" is what her father had said to her mother. "It's an abomination."

Mama walked fast. We had trouble keeping up with her, and soon she was far ahead of us, her slippers slapping loudly against the concrete. Noon reached out and took my hand, squeezed it, and I returned the gesture. Mama broke into a light trot then. Without turning around, she told us to meet her at the hospital. I had never seen Mama run before.

When Noon and I arrived at the hospital, I was surprised to find that we were still holding hands. "It's going to be all right," Noon said at the door, letting go. It was almost one in the morning; the hospital was empty except for a few orderlies flitting in and out of the hallway. When we got to the front desk, the receptionist looked up and said, "Room 451," as though she'd been waiting all night for us to arrive.

I panicked. For some reason, the room number made everything intolerably real to me, even as the world suddenly became charged with a strange, dreamlike quality: Colors became impossibly bright, the slightest sound boomed raucously, the air became a thick, coppery substance on my tongue. I felt myself hover about like a ghoul. Inside the elevator, the fluorescents buzzing loudly above us, I felt as if Noon and I were falling quickly through an infinite cavern, though I knew the contraption was taking us up to the fourth floor. Noon was saying something to me, but when I looked at her lips, they moved quickly and soundlessly, like a movie on fast-forward, and I wanted to ask her why she'd want to play tricks on me now.

The door to Room 451 was ajar. It was dark inside. I looked in and saw Papa laid out with bandages wrapped around his temple. A morphine drip ticked at his side, its tubes like the shadow of some gangly tree. Mama sat beside him on the gurney, a hand on his thigh, staring into his sleeping face, which winced intermittently as if he were deep in some strange and painful dream. Mama didn't look up when we arrived. She just kept staring at Papa's face, mesmerized by his features. She was still winded from running. I watched her collarbone tilt back and forth beneath her nightgown. I walked into the room. Noon remained in the doorway.

I reached over and turned on the light beside the hospital gurney. Mama put her forearm up to her eyes. In his sleep, Papa stirred as well. Under the light, his face was a pale shade of lavender. He turned over, revealing a thick bandage on the side of his head, drenched purple and black with blood, the cloth matted with the substance. I felt relieved then, as Papa turned away, and even as the stench of the bloodied bandage filled my nostrils. It smelled like that flatbed full of dead chickens, and I thought about how blood was blood no matter if it's from a chicken or a man. But at least he was alive, and, thinking this, I felt the world become coherent again.

Mama was saying something. For a second, I thought my ears were still playing tricks on me: I heard only garbling and mewing. But then I saw Noon's face in the doorway and realized from the way she tilted her head that the sounds coming from my mother's lips were incomprehensible to her as well. "Mama," I said, and she looked at me stunned, as if she didn't recognize me, didn't even know I had been standing there. She squinted and gestured for me to turn off the lamp. The room fell into darkness again. Mama touched Papa's thigh once more, rubbed it, cinched the fabric of his hospital gown as if she were testing the quality of the material for one of her bras.

"Can you believe it?" Mama said, and from the sound of her voice I could not tell if she was laughing or crying. "Ladda, can you believe it?" I stood there beside her, watched my father's ribs moving slowly against his hospital gown, his face still wincing every so often. "Can you believe it, Ladda?" Mama asked again, this time in a singsong voice, and I wanted to ask her what I was supposed to be incredulous about, but when I opened my mouth to speak, nothing came out, just a few short, exasperated breaths. As in the elevator a few minutes earlier, I felt like I was falling into a bottomless pit, that the room had been dropped into a chasm, and I wanted desperately to turn on the bedside lamp, for I thought light might put an end to the nausea. I felt weightless even as I felt my limbs weighted with a thousand dumbbells anchored to the floor. The room began to tilt and turn around me. I held on to the gurney rail for balance. "Can you believe it, Ladda?"

Mama said once more. This time she cackled as if she'd never understood how funny the question was. "How could they?"

I walked toward Mama, raised my right hand high into the air, and brought it down upon the side of her face. For a split second, before I hit her, Mama jutted her chin out and looked at me as if she wanted—needed—to receive the blow, had been hoping I would do this all along. The impact barely made a noise, nor did it seem to have much of an effect: It only turned her head around, like something strange had caught her attention. She looked disappointed—not because I had hit her, but because I had not hit her hard enough—so I raised my hand and hit her once more, this time with more force, squarely on the bridge of her nose. I wanted her to ward off my blows. I wanted her to fight back. But she just sat there as if she not only had expected my blows, but needed more fury to stir her to life. "Don't you go crazy on me," I yelled. "Stop talking like a fucking lunatic. Make some goddamn sense, Mama."

Noon grabbed me. Mama laughed again, high-pitched and girlish, a light trail of blood trickling from her left nostril. I lunged at her again, but Noon had her arms tight around my body. "Ladda, don't," Noon whispered into my ear. "Enough."

I realized then that Mama wasn't laughing—she was crying. Her shoulders were not shaking with mad, devilish hilarity; they were trembling with grief. She dabbed at her bleeding nostril with the base of her thumb. When she saw the blood, she got up and walked toward Noon and me. Noon still had me in her arms. Mama's silhouette seemed surprisingly large before me then. I looked up at her, and seeing her swollen eyes, looked down at my feet. Noon walked out and closed the door behind her.

It was my turn now, I thought, staring at the floor, feeling my mother's breath on my shoulders. I would let Mama punish me as I had thought I was punishing her. I would jut out my chin to receive her hand. And, that done, I would let her do it again and again and again until she was at long last satisfied. But she didn't. All she did was tell me they had cut off Papa's ear. They took everything, she said. Little Jui and his goons. All the lobe and all the cartilage and everything else that goes with an ear. All they'd left was a nub and a hole on the side of his head. Mama dabbed her nostrils with the hem of her blouse and walked out of the room. I listened to her slippers trailing off down the hall. I looked at the gurney. Papa had turned over once more. He stared at me astonished, the white of his eyes like jewels in the dark. And in a dazed, whispering voice that told me he was still very much asleep, swimming in his morphine dream, my father said: "Yes. Yes. Yes. A hundred and a thousand times yes already."

XVIII

The days in the hospital were long. I don't think Mama slept the whole four days. She sat in an armchair beside the gurney, staring back and forth between Papa and the window over-looking the hospital parking lot. I tried to talk to her, but she'd only nod at me or shake her head, as if I'd uttered nothing but questions. She didn't eat. I would get food from the cafeteria, but she would only nibble at it courteously before setting down the tray. She never mentioned the fact that I'd hit her; after a while, her silence seemed punishment enough. Noon came by to pick me up for school every morning, but I couldn't bring myself to leave Papa's side, and Mama didn't seem to mind.

Papa woke up every so often. He never said a word. He would look at us, stare at the ceiling, click his morphine drip, and just wait for sleep to come again. We both tried to speak to him, but he'd simply turn over onto his side. Doctors in neatly pressed lab coats would come into the room. The in-fection was beginning to heal, they said on the second day, which explained the stench at night.

Nurses came in twice a day to change Papa's bandage and clean his wound. That was the only time Papa ever made a sound. Mama would stand and look calmly over the nurses' shoulders. I didn't want to see the wound; it was enough to see the nurses wince.

We received some flowers and cards, but nobody came to visit. It was as if people were afraid that they might be put-ting themselves in harm's way, as though Papa's unfortunate fate was a contractible disease.

On the evening of the second day, Noon came by and we climbed onto the hospital roof. She'd brought iced coffee and cigarettes. The town stretched below us; on the horizon, we could see the hills that separated us from our neighbors to the north. I tried to find our property, but I couldn't see much beyond the rubber grove on the eastern side of the roof. It occurred to me then that Mama and I had not gone back to the house since we'd left. I wondered if the strays were smart enough to notice our absence. Perhaps they would go to the chicken house first and then, upon finding no sustenance there, move to the house itself.

Noon told me she'd seen Little Jui around town driving Papa's Mazda.

"It's a crime, Ladda," Noon said. "It's an abomination what they did to your father. You should report it to the police."

I shook my head. I reminded Noon that the chief of our esteemed police department was Big Jui's brother-in-law. Given the way things worked in our town, Papa'd get arrested for having his own ear cut off. Papa lost, I reminded Noon. He bet more than he could afford. The police would probably say that an ear was the least Papa could give for a bet he never meant to pay. "Still," Noon replied, sighing, "that doesn't make it right, Ladda," and I said she should know by now that we were living in a world where words like that didn't mean a thing: right or wrong, left or right, up or down, inside or outside—our people didn't speak that kind of language.

We took Papa home on the fourth day. Miss Mayuree sent one of her men over with the sedan and for the first time I did not feel any rancor toward her. Miss Mayuree told Mama that she could keep to her old quota for the time being, eight hundred bras a month. Mama thanked her once again. The nub on Papa's head had stopped bleeding now, though there remained a large square bandage taped over the side of his scalp. When we got home, Mama sat Papa on the front porch, cleaned out the wound, changed the bandage. Papa grimaced as she swabbed the wound with alcohol, but still he didn't say a thing. The doctors had advised vigilance—they said the infection might spread. I couldn't bear to look at Papa's wound, so I carried my bags to my bedroom and left Mama and Papa on the porch.

For the first time in a while, I felt calm. It was as if I'd expended all my anger that first night in the hospital, hitting Mama, screaming at her. Nor did I feel any anguish for what happened to Papa. What happened happened, I decided, and I could see no use in wishing that it didn't. The doctors told us that Papa would still be able to hear out of both ears—only the cartilage had been taken—which really was the most anybody could hope for, they said. They made Little Jui's barbarity seem perversely generous.

At breakfast the next morning, Papa spoke for the first time. Over porridge, he said, "This is delicious," and Mama and I looked at him astonished, for I think in some ways we'd been preparing for the possibility that he might never speak again.

"What?" Papa said, grinning at us both. "You guys don't think it's delicious?"

We slowly started speaking again. In steady increments, there was talk in the house once more. There was kindness. There was generosity. There was laughing and smiling and even, at times, delight. Mama and Papa decided to plant a garden in the yard—zinnias and azaleas and birds-of-paradise and morning glories. I'd come home from school and see them out there bent over the earth together, the sun casting its long rays, and if it hadn't been for that square bandage over Papa's missing ear, you would've thought we were as normal as anybody else. The strays would emerge at night to inspect the garden, pause to sniff the budding flowers. And if it hadn't been for that chicken house, with its empty coops and bags of premium feed lining the mud walls, you never would've guessed that my father once fought chickens as though nothing else mattered.

I'd occasionally see Little Jui in town with his bodyguards and Ramon. I'd walk the other way. He never bothered me again. It was as though he'd decided to move on to other, more entertaining game. I'd heard that many of the men had stopped going to the cockpit after what Little Jui did to my father. It was the end of cockfighting in our town. Dog racing was the new game: Saksri Bualoi had retired undefeated as the welterweight champion of the world and opened up a world-class dog track in his hometown. It was something else, the rumormongers said, to sit there in the stands and eat marinated porkballs and drink fifths of rye and watch those beautiful dogs run.

XIX

We went back to the hospital for a checkup later that month. Everything's fine, the doctor told us, peering sternly into the bandage. No infection. Good progress all around. He recommended a prosthetic for Papa. "It will be easy," he said. "All we need to do is make a mold of your other ear." He pulled out a few dummies from a leather suitcase—an ear, a nose, a shin, a hand, a foot, all made from some complicated sounding substance, all tinted the same pinkish hue. The doctor put the artificial ear in Papa's hand. Papa fingered it and said, "Why, it's just rubber, Doctor," and the doctor shrugged as if he couldn't be bothered to explain again. "I don't need a rubber ear," Papa said, laughing, handing the prosthetic back. "Thanks but no thanks. Lots of ugly people in this world, Doctor. And they're no less ugly for having two ears on their heads." The doctor nodded, looked at his watch. Before we left, he took off Papa's bandage. I looked at Papa's wound for the first time: the bulging, translucent half-moon of scar tissue; the short brown notch which the doctor called the tragus; the small hole that made me think of some flesh-eating creature burrowing itself deep into the side of Papa's head. Papa walked to the mirror. "It's not so bad," I said, and Papa smiled at me appreciatively.

That night, I went into the chicken house after dinner. I hadn't been in there since the day I told Papa about Little Jui coming to take the Mazda. It still smelled strongly of chicken shit and stale urine. A few sparrows had made their home in the thatch roof, getting fat off the remaining bags of chicken feed. They fluttered around as I entered the chicken house. I didn't light the lantern. I just sat down in the dark and listened to the sounds around me: the hum of Mama's sewing machine on the front porch; Papa watering the garden, long jets of water beating an irregular rhythm against the soil; the sparrows chirping overhead; the cicadas singing in the trees; the strays lifting their voices in turn to join that insect orchestra. I sat there for a long time, until Mama and Papa went inside. Mama turned on the kitchen light and the chicken-house windows cupped its yellow rays. I watched her shadow moving on the chicken-house floor. Soon, she turned off the light and I was in darkness again. I heard my parents murmuring and then I heard their bedroom door shut. I could sense nothing then of my parents, nothing of the house, just the noises the animals made. After a while, even the animals seemed to go to sleep, as though all the world had decided to turn in with my parents for the night, and I held my breath because it seemed the only sound left in the world and all around me then was an extraordinary silence. It made me feel light, that silence, as if I might float to the ceiling, as if I might be able to open my arms, flap them, and fly with the sparrows. I don't know how long I sat there holding my breath in the dark, but I thought then of how loud the world could be, so much clatter and noise, and of how lovely and rare was a moment like this when one need not listen to anything at all.

A truck motor rumbled down the road, coughing and sputtering sporadically. I got up and walked out, decided to turn in for the night. But when I walked across the yard, I noticed that it was Papa's Mazda coming toward the house. I paused, hoping they wouldn't see me. The truck approached, its headlights throwing wild shadows against the rubber trees. I hoped they'd simply pass me by. They did. But then, just as I stepped onto the front porch, the Mazda stopped. The truck began to back up toward our property. It stopped at the entrance to our driveway.

The driver got out of the car. He started walking toward me, his shadow growing in size, the gravel crunching beneath his feet. At first, I wanted to go inside the house. But then I thought I might say a thing or two to Little Jui. I thought I might give him a piece of my mind. He was alone; there were three of us here. This was our property. If he gave me any trouble, Mama and Papa would come out. I sat down on the porch steps and waited for him.

"What do you want?" I shouted, but he didn't respond, just kept on walking toward me. "Speak up, motherfucker."

But, again, no response, only his huffing louder with the closing distance. He was some ten meters away when the moon came out from behind a cloud. By its blue light, I saw that he was not Little Jui at all but that Filipino boy Ramon.

I was afraid now. I'd expected Little Jui—I'd been prepared to confront him once and for all—but I hadn't expected

Ramon. He must've sensed my fear and surprise, because he slowed his pace, held his hands before him as though to say he meant me no harm. I stood up. I could smell his sweat now. I could've touched his face. He smiled. I turned to go back inside the house, but Ramon reached out and grabbed my hand.

"What do you want?" I whispered, turning to face him, struggling against his grip. His hand felt cold, clammy against my skin. "Go away," I whispered, and when he smiled at me again, I noticed for the first time his swollen right brow, a messy trail of dried blood branching across his cheek in every direction. He let go of my hand, and though I wanted to turn back to the house, I kept staring into his battered face, mesmerized by the ganglia of blood on his cheek. He said something, but it was in another language—Tagalog, perhaps—and I shook my head to tell him I didn't understand. He said something again, the same guttural phrase, his voice a dim whisper between us. I shook my head again. "I don't understand," I said, and for the first time I saw how helpless he actually was—this foreign boy cast into a foreign land to handle other people's chickens—and I wondered what had happened tonight to produce those bruises on his face, where he'd been headed in the Mazda before he saw me. He opened his mouth to say something again, but then he took one of my wrists into his hand, as if the gesture might explain what he'd been trying to say. I didn't resist this time. For a moment, it seemed like Ramon was taking my pulse, his fingers hot against my veins.

He reached into the pocket of his jeans. He put something in my hand. He closed my fingers around the object.

"What is this?" I asked, holding up my fist, my fingers hugging the object's cold, velvety texture. He shrugged. I already knew what it was. I already knew what he'd given me; I didn't have to open my fingers to see. I didn't want it. "What is this?" I asked again, but Ramon turned around and started walking back toward the Mazda. I caught up with him. He stopped.

"I don't want it," I said. I tried to take one of his hands, return the strange token, but he pulled away and shook his head. He said something to me again in that guttural language. I stared at him. The object felt heavy in my hands, like a warm mushroom, and I realized then that I was squeezing it hard. He reached out, put a hand on my cheek, said something once more. He gestured with his chin toward the Mazda. He pointed toward my house. He put a palm over his heart. I shook my head. "I don't understand," I said. "I don't understand what you want." He repeated the gestures once more—the Mazda, the house, his heart—and this time, for some reason, I thought I understood him.

He wanted to go home.

"Help," he said loudly in Thai, and for a moment I stared at him dumbfounded, Papa's flesh still hot in my fist. "Help," he said again. "Me."

He walked to the Mazda. He got in the passenger seat. He sat there for a long time staring at me, waiting. I knew then what I needed to do. I crouched down and started digging a small hole through the gravel driveway with one hand, my fingers still wrapped around Papa's ear in the other. The ground beneath the gravel was hard, and I felt soil collecting in my fingernails. The hardened topsoil soon gave way to softer mulch, and I clawed at it furiously, grabbing fistfuls of dirt. I thought I might be able to sit there digging in that driveway forever.

I dropped Papa's ear into that hole and covered it up with clumps of cold gravel. I stood up and walked toward the Mazda. I got in the driver's seat. I rolled down the window. "Let's go," I muttered, popping the truck into gear, and then I was gone.

ACKNOWLEDGMENTS

Thanks are due to many individuals and institutions for their invaluable support and encouragement. This book would not exist without the following believers.

Siriwan Sriboonyapirat. Wannasiri Lapcharoensap. June Glasson. Nancy Lee and Julien Victor Koschmann. Sorachai Buasap. Kawin Punchangthong. Daniel Mrozowski. Jean Henry. Michael Cobb. Hong-an Tran. Cheryl Beredo. Kate Rubin. Charles Baxter, Eileen Pollack, Nancy Reisman, Reginald McKnight, Peter Ho Davies, and Nicholas Delbanco at the University of Michigan creative writing program. My fellow writers in Ann Arbor—Laura Jean Baker, John Bishop, Andrew Cohen, Melodie Edwards, Sara Houghteling, Laura Krughoff, John Lee, Patti Lu, David Morse, Michelle Mounts, and Catherine Zeidler. Lexy Bloom. Fatema Ahmed and Matt Weiland at *Granta*. Tamara Straus and Michael Ray at *Zoetrope: All-Story*. Linda Swanson-Davies at *Glimmer Train*. John Kulka, Natalie Danford, and Francine Prose. The Avery Jules Hopwood Awards Program. The Fred R. Meijer Fellowship in Creative Writing, which provided instrumental funds.

The indomitable Amy Williams and the wonderful people at Collins-McCormick. Elisabeth Schmitz, Morgan Entrekin, Dara Hyde, Lauren Wein, Charles Rue Woods, and the incredible staff at Grove/Atlantic, Inc. Thank you all.

This book is also dedicated to the memory of Sucheng Tang—beloved *ahmah*—who crossed the South China Sea to an uncertain future in Bangkok seventy years ago and who is now, without doubt, enjoying bird's nest soup in a much better world than the one she inherited.